# BOYS' TOWN

### Art Bosch

Boston • Alyson Publications, Inc.

Published as a trade paperback original by
Alyson Publications
40 Plympton St.
Boston, Mass. 02118.

Distributed in the U.K. by GMP Publishers,
PO Box 247, London, N15 6RW, England.

First U.S. edition: June, 1988

ISBN 1-55583-126-5
LC 87-072875

For *the boys*:
Bill Becraft, Art Rodriguez,
Max Talavera, John Alexander,
Efren Valadez and Ray Alvarez.

The distinction between what is real and what is imaginary is not one that can be finally maintained ... all existing things are, in an intelligible sense, imaginary.
        —John S. MacKenzie


The only *unnatural* thing in life, is doing what doesn't come naturally.
        —Nash Aquilon


Serious gay men are like truffles: they're around, but you have to dig for them!
        —Scout deYoung

# 1. Some Enchanted Evening

It was the kind of look that Cinderella might have flashed old Prince Charming, after a few years of living happily ever after. The comic hybrid of a grimace and a smirk. The kind of look Ricky was forever giving Lucy. It was an expression Nash Aquilon used not infrequently with his thirty-year-old best friend and housemate, Scout deYoung.

"Loosen up, Scout," he complained, razzing his alter ego from the bathroom door. "Jesus, you look like *Donny Osmond*!"

Scout whipped off his tie. "I do not!"

"You do. Just look at yourself."

"I am," he said, studying the reflection in the mirror. "If I look like anyone it's Tom Cruise or Jan-Michael Vincent with dark hair and glasses."

Nash gaffawed, causing a tattooed panther on his left bicep to crouch inward toward a pair of classically chiseled pectorals. "You wish. Try one of the Hardy Boys."

"Why don't you — you've *tried* everyone else!"

Nash grinned, unruffled. Scout was always attacking his sexual proclivities. "I don't get it."

"Ha! Tell that to half the population of Boys' Town."

He ignored the innuendo. "No, I mean, why do you insist on looking like Clark Kent, when you have Superman potential? Don't you think it's about time you got rid of those funky horn-rimmed glasses and invested in some contact lenses?"

After composing himself, Scout turned to him dead-pan. "There's a lawn sprinkler in the front yard. Why don't you sit on it and rotate? Pretend it's a dildo!"

"Hey, crack jokes. I'm just trying to help. If you want to look like Rex Reed, that's your business."

Exasperated, Scout reached for his cigarettes — the Surgeon General was making an emergency call to his lungs. He'd already changed his clothes three times, and to his complete dissatisfaction, his housemate was right. The reflection in the mirror still resembled what Nash jokingly referred to as his book-of-the-month-gay-recluse-librarian look. He subscribed to *GQ*, but the print from the pages was the only thing that had rubbed off.

Nash fanned the smoke from his face. "You smoke too much."

A cigarette bobbed between Scout's lips as he spoke. "It's my only vice — give me a break." He removed his tie again.

"That and romancing the bone. So, where are you going?"

"Ted and Justine's for dinner."

He flinched. "Jesus, I'd rather stay home and stick pins in my eyes. I could think of better things to do with myself than wasting an evening with *those* two."

"I can imagine. Like rounding up your gym buddies for an old-fashioned nipple-piercing party!"

Nash fingered the diamond stud in his ear lobe. He'd never told Scout about the time he almost fainted when one of his ex-boyfriends pierced his ear. Nipples were definitely out.

"Why don't you do something constructive for a change?"

"Yeah. Like what?"

"You could proofread that article I finished for *Jock* magazine: 'Cross-country Cruising and RV Maintenance.'"

Turning right off of Dicks (a street name of queer coincidence, Scout assured himself, that had nothing to do with the decided sexual preferences of the area residents, but nevertheless, like Boys' Town's zip code, which ended in 69, helped solidify his growing belief that he was experiencing life through the eyes of M. C. Escher), he walked south to Santa Monica Boulevard.

Before turning left at Bank of America, he glanced back toward the birds of paradise that flocked around the two-bedroom stucco which he and Nash called home. Once a wreck of a house, it had now been transformed to semi-*Architectural Digest* beauty by their sense of gay aesthetics and hard cash that would never be reimbursed. No wonder landlords preferred renting to gays. Gays not only respected the property, they increased its value in the process.

A brief detour took him to the San Vicenti post office where he deposited a hundred envelopes in the STAMPS ONLY box.

Ted and Justine were unlike any of Scout's other friends. But, then, they weren't actually friends. Not true friends that could be roused from a dead sleep at three without explaining the Who What When and Where (notably the Who) of the situation. If he thought of them at all, it was as genetically altered Ken and Barbie dolls, who had jumped on the latest vogue and overdosed. Stylish pseudo-punks. Ted had the requisite health spa physique, natty Young Republican looks and an ultra-square Abercrombie & Fitch wardrobe that produced a punk effect in reverse.

Justine, a spastic antithesis of her husband, looked like a freaked-out Ophelia in post-nuclear drag, with padded NFL shoulders, guerilla make-up and a wild-child bouffant that seemed to have tangled with a vacuum cleaner and lost.

Still, they were an alternative to an otherwise mundane evening of TV reruns, boiling bag entrees, and what Nash referred to as his penchant for *doodling his noodle*.

Tonight, Justine looked like a psycho Annie Hall. "For me?" she squealed like a goosed macaw.

In her own inimitable way, she looked resplendent in a sour orange tiger-print jumpsuit that cuffed pedal pusher-style around zebraskin pantyhose.

"T'ain't nothin'," Scout smiled, presenting her with an exotic bouquet. Justine's affinity for flowers (especially the plastic ones Woolworth's sold in the fifties) was well known among her friends. She grabbed the bouquet as he stepped across the threshold of their home, which was a tribute in bad taste to an era they were all too young to remember. It looked like a Denny's on a bad night.

Justine plucked a flower from the bouquet and planted it in a hairdo that looked as if it had been constructed with Krazy Glue. The flower was a perfect match for a vermilion streak jettisoning from the left side of her skull. Scout watched in amazement as she pirouetted across shiny hardwood floors toward the kitchen on perilously high stiletto heels — a fashion victim if ever there was one.

Ted waved from an old new-wave sofa in the adjoining room where he was conversing with a good-looking man in a corduroy sport coat and jeans. The man's bushy moustache and sun-streaked brown hair sent a murmur of recognition through Scout's heart. Then it clicked. He'd seen him there before with a sloe-eyed beauty that looked like she had just arrived from a cover shoot for *Harper's Bazaar*. He couldn't remember their names, but he did remember that they were married. He wondered where she was tonight.

"Calistoga with a twist. Right?" Ted cocked his thumb and index finger pistol-like at Scout's chest.

Nodding, Scout suddenly realized how *gay* it sounded, and he hadn't even said it. While Ted fixed his drink, he prayed that he wouldn't be introduced as their gay-writer-friend. He hated being the token gay — it was so sixties. Luckily, the guest beat him to the draw.

"Hi, Scout. I don't know if you remember me, we met here once before. I'm Jesse Youngblood."

Flattered that he'd been remembered, Scout cordially accepted the hand with a good-natured smile. It was hard and calloused with an unmistakable gold band around the marriage finger. He gave it his butchest tug.

"Scout's our gay-writer-friend," Ted beamed, handing Scout his drink.

Scout's smile curdled. He wished he could twink his nose like Samantha the witch and produce a large, sharp machete. Ted's knees would be the first to go.

"Jesse's a carpenter," Ted continued, settling on the ugly sofa of oversized cabbage roses and aqua Naugahyde.

Jesse shrugged, forcing a smile in Ted's direction.

Their heads turned in unison as Justine clicked into the room carrying a sterling platter of freshly nuked hors d'oeuvres. Wobbling slightly, she managed to place them delicately on the coffee table that resembled a cartoon prop from *The Jetsons*. Then, on dagger heels, she disappeared into the kitchen.

"Justine's not herself tonight," Ted smiled apologetically.

"I'll say," Scout said innocently, wondering if she was ever herself. "Is it the *curse* or what?"

Jesse choked on a steaming hors d'oeuvre.

"No, it's not *that*," Ted said snidely, gulping his cocktail. "Fifi and Miles's Mercedes broke down in Palm Springs — they canceled. Then, Baxter and Crystal called from San Francisco. All the planes are fogged in. So, poor Justine's sailing the high seas of Cutty Sark tonight."

"Well," Scout drawled, "my mama always said that if God had wanted us to fly, we'da been born with Samsonite!"

A wicked smile crossed Jesse's lips as he winked to Scout from across the room.

Ted wasn't amused. "Well," he covered, "Justine's so high-strung about her little dinner parties." He quickly fixed himself another drink, trying to maintain his sense of cool. "You know Justine. The show must go on."

He didn't know how right he was. As if on cue, a blood-curdling scream reverberated through the house. The three men raced to the kitchen.

Justine was sprawled spread-eagle across the Congoleum, sobbing uncontrollably. She looked like something a Cuisinart had pureed, then spit across the floor.

Ted sprung to his knees. "Honey, what is it?"

*What is it?* Scout thought Ted's brains must have been made by Mattel. It took him less than a second to surmise the situation: Justine, drunk on her ass, had obviously fallen from her ridiculously high heels and twisted, if not broken, her ankle.

"Get me to St. John's," she shrieked. "I'm dying, you asshole!"

Jesse and Scout manuevered her outside as the asshole scurried for their industrial strength beige BMW. Squealing radials left them marooned on the sidewalk as Ted burned rubber in the general direction of the hospital.

Jesse elbowed Scout. "Wait'll the nuns get a load of her," he grinned conspiratorially.

Scout's arm was high above his head, motioning elegantly in perfect imitation of the Queen of England's royal wave.

"I think everyone should have at least one friend who's a Cyndi Lauper look-alike," he winked. "Don't you?"

## 2. What's for Dessert?

Delores was a flashback to the Eisenhower era; a nostalgic stroll down memory lane; a megadose of fifties deja vu for baby-boom adults. It was also the only *authentic* drive-in restaurant in the Boy's Town area with bobby-soxed carhops, menus with connecting metal speakers, and the best chili cheeseburgers and double malteds west of the San Andreas Fault. And, it was the place where Scout and Jesse ended up eating after the fiasco at Ted and Justine's.

While Scout studied the carpenter's face under the flourescent glow of Delores's lights, outside the carhops were hopping cars for donations to save it. Little did they know it was a lost cause. Delores (like love and all good things) would reach an untimely demise. Those old kissin' cousins, Progress and Economics, would raze her like a chili cheeseburger beneath the steel-belted wheels of dollar signs and merged interests. Money not only spoke a universal language, but invariably got its way. So, without so much as a wink of regret, Money dug her spiked green heels into Delores and kicked up a multi-million dollar Savings & Loan, convincing carhops and their loyal clientele that Simone Signoret knew of what she spoke: "Nostalgia ain't what it used to be."

But before Delores's sad fate was reached and her chili cheeseburgers sank into the dank bowels of progress, Scout and Jesse savored her greasy culinary delights.

Between bites of a burger and sips of a vanilla malt, Scout contemplated his companion's considerable charms. There were sexy lines under his eyes that extended to high, chiseled cheek-bones when he laughed or smiled. His face had a lived-in quality to it. It looked the way a man's face ought to look, without benefit of creams and emollients and vain promises from beauty jars on medicine chest shelves.

Too bad, he thought, shifting his attention to the band of gold around Jesse's finger. It never failed. The good ones were either already taken or blissfully heterosexual.

"I'm stuffed," Jesse groaned, pushing a greasy paper plate toward the center of the table.

Scout lit a cigarette. "Me too. I think we lucked out tonight. Did you see Justine's hors d'oeuvres?"

"Did I — I ate one of them!"

"Man, her microwave must be turbo-charged. Those suckers practically glowed."

Jesse chuckled. "How'd you like to come over for a drink? Or some coffee? It's still early."

"Actually," Scout lied, "there's an old Bette Davis movie on TV that I wanted to watch. Maybe another time." He didn't think he could handle seeing Jesse with his glamorous wife in their undoubtedly tasteful home. Why rub salt on the wound?

"We have a TV. We could watch it together."

Scout stalled. "Gee, I've got some writing to do, too."

Jesse reached across the table and touched Scout's hand. "C'mon."

Scout froze, but quickly recovered. "Are you and your wife into three-ways or maybe you thought Ted's gay-writer-friend would blow something other than your mind?"

"What? No! Hey, I don't think you understand. It's just me and Jackson, but he should be asleep by now."

Scout was visibly confused. "Let me get this *straight*. You're married, but you're living with a guy named Jackson, but it's okay to bring me home because *he's* asleep? Jesus, and they say gays are kinky. Man, you bisexuals really take the cake. Talk about wanton!"

People were beginning to stare. "Hey, calm down."

"No way, José!" Scout made tracks out the door.

Jesse quickly threw a tip on the table and zoomed out after him. "Hey, wait a second!"

Scout paused long enough for a hand to come from behind and grasp his shoulder. He quickly brushed it off, then turned on Jesse, full face. A mean sneer bristled his moustache. He looked like he was going to spit.

Jesse sighed. "Hey, I'm gay, Scout."

He knew a straight line when he heard one, and went for it like Bette Davis in heat. "Ha! That's cute — does your *wife* know?" He felt meaner than Rosa Moline in *Beyond The Forest*.

"Yeah. As a matter of fact, she does. We're divorced."

The egg on Scout's face started a slow slide. He felt like the last fool. "Jesus, you mean you weren't suggesting a three-way?"

"Are you disappointed?" he smiled.

"No. Not at all. Jeeze, you must think I'm the last pervert or something."

"Aside from an overzealous imagination, I'd bet that you're a pretty nice fellow."

A sheepish smile curled Scout's moustache.

"I almost bowed out of Ted and Justine's little *soirée* this evening. Now I'm glad I didn't."

"Well, then. That puts an entirely different light on the subject."

"C'mon. Let's go get that coffee." His smile was a welcome mat of invitation.

Scout held back. "All right, but there's just one other thing."

"What's that?"

"Who's Jackson? Your lover?"

Jesse stuck both hands in his pockets and looked to the sky. "Jackson's my son. He's in my custody. I haven't lived with my wife in over a year. I'm self-employed. I'm thirty-three years old. Let's see..."

"Hey, I don't want to pry."

"Pry away. I have a distinct feeling that you'd only imagine the worst, otherwise."

"Hey, you've only been gay a year — there's a lot to learn between the hardcore and the pretty."

"Well, there's one thing you should know about me. I don't have time for games. All right?"

*All Right* — it was music to his ears; like Chaka Khan on a bluesy high note; Eugene Ormandy and the Philadelphia Orchestra; all five octaves of the incredible Patti LaBelle; shoot, it was raindrops on roses and whiskers on kittens.

"I'm sorry. I guess I'm overly cautious. My mama always said, 'Scout, know which side your bread is buttered on before you eat it.'"

"I like your mama. Couldn't you tell I'm gay?"

"Who can tell anymore? Gays aren't the only ones with sculptured physiques nowadays. Shoot, even the straights look gay." He laughed at the thought. "Who would've thought that machismo would one day embrace blow dryers and lite beer?"

They left on the threshold of a new friendship. Each was hoping for the best, wishing on a night star that this one was the right one. It wasn't easy in a town where the *right one* was as rare as a blue unicorn in a herd of mustangs.

# 3. Who — What — When — Where

Scout arrived home a little past ten the following morning. As he was coming up the sidewalk a brutally handsome platinum blond, with Slavic cheekbones and a body that was a living advertisement for free weights and forced rep's, was exiting from their front door.

Bounding athletically across the front yard, he leaped into a black Jeep and was gone before Scout reached the house.

Inside, Nash was waiting for him at the kitchen table like a butch Mary Worth.

"You're up early," Scout yawned, deliberately avoiding Nash's eyes.

"When you didn't come home last night, I sat up worrying."

Scout rolled his eyes. "If you were up all night it was because of that Polykleitos mass of muscles I just saw leaving the house."

Nash's face lit up. "Yeah. Did you get a look at those Winnebagoes? If Dolly Parton was a man, they could pass for twins." He reached for the morning paper as his eyebrows shimmied up and down his forehead. "And, how was *your* night? Did you trick?"

Scout cringed. He hated that particular word in the gay lexicon, especially so early in the morning.

Nash stared at him. "So, does he rim on the first date?"

"Give me a break, Nash."

"That bad, huh?"

"I'd rather not discuss it, all right?"

"Now, don't be that way," he teased. "I want a blow-by-blow account. Just pretend you're Jackie Collins."

Scout wasn't talking.

"Come on. At least up to the disgusting part. I want the Who What When and Where! It's not every night the Poster Boy for Celibacy ventures out into the real world, then doesn't return until the next morning. Something had to happen." Patting the chair beside him, he motioned Scout over to the kitchen table for the 411. "Now, you tell Miss Rona all about it."

Scout was mute as a Sphinx.

"At least tell me what he does for a living."

Scout hedged, thinking it over. "He's a carpenter."

"How fuckin' butch! Mine bends hair in Beverly Hills."

"A hairdresser?" He laughed. "Are you kidding me? With a body like that I would've thought he lifted office buildings for a living."

"So, tell me about your carpenter. Did he know how to use his *tool*?"

"You're sick!"

"Come on. Was it bigger than a two-by-four?"

"I mean it, Nash."

"Did his *drill* work?"

"Stop it."

"Ah, come on, Scout. Sex is just your emotions in motion; a medium for your libido to creatively express itself. It's a free art form. Your problem is that your canvas has been blank so long you've forgotten how to use your brush."

"Spoken like the sexual freelancer that you are."

Nash sipped his coffee. "Well, it's true."

Scout smiled patiently. "You know, Nash," he began, sounding like the high school English teacher he once was, "contrary to what you may have heard, the measure of another man's worth is not calculated by what's hanging between his thighs."

Nash whistled. "That bad, huh?"

"You're incorrigibly *gay*!"

"And proud of it, too, pal."

Scout took a seat at the kitchen table, lowering his voice to a conspiratorial whisper. "The secret to life cannot be found in the rotary dexterity of another man's pelvis, Nash."

"Bullshit, Socrates!" He'd been taken. "All I want is a bit of morning conversation."

"All right. We could discuss Rousseau's criteria for a moral life — from the gay perspective, of course."

"I was thinking more along the lines of vital statistics. Get my drift?"

"Loud and clear."

"Come on, Scout. I tell *you* all the time."

"In graphic detail — but I never *ask!*"

"Up yours!" Flipping the morning paper in front of his face, Nash sulkily studied the day's horoscopes.

"Listen, he's a really nice man, but you know me — since when do I fornicate on the first date, much less *have* a first date?"

That seemed to assuage Nash's piqued pride. Scout never could relate to generic sex, and when it came to discussing his sex life, he was the Greta Garbo of the heart. "And, whose fault is that? If you'd spend a little more time living life instead of writing about it, you'd score more often. You have to circulate."

"I'm not into meat rack socializing. Now, tell me about this blond Adonis hairdresser — *I'm asking!*"

"In a minute. Listen to your horoscope: 'Aries: Be ready for a new lease on love. Events need a push. An exciting twist develops with a lover.' Hey, I knew you wouldn't be an old maid all your life. It says right here in black and white — 'Events need a push.'"

He chewed his bottom lip. "I don't believe in that stuff. Besides, I don't even have a lover."

"See — that's what I mean. Maybe this carpenter guy is the lover with an exciting twist."

"Do you think..."

"Who knows. It sure as hell has to beat the sound of one hand *wacking* night after night after night ... Now, about this hairdresser."

Scout fixed a smile on his face and listened. After all, he'd asked.

# 4. New Kid in Town

Twenty-one-year-old Buddy Dove, a rare Portuguese blond from Muncie, Indiana, took to Boy's Town, West Hollywood, like bubblegum takes to the soles of pedestrianism.

It hit him as soon as he deplaned at LAX. Something was in the air that wasn't discernible in Indiana, and it wasn't just the hazy halo of smog — the flatulence of a city on wheels, where walking was on the same level as balancing the national budget — it just wasn't done.

After the bigoted pretense and prejudice of Indiana, it was like awakening to a surreal dream by Fritz Lang. A Technicolor *Metropolis*, with the added sensation of sound.

As he cruised his rent-a-car into West Hollywood, into the preternatural shine of smog-filtered sunlight, he no longer felt *different*. He felt like one of the Boys, comfortably at home. It was like a breath of fresh air, even if the air was brown. He knew then that the chances of returning to the small college community, to his job waiting table at the Carriage House — the classiest restaurant in Muncie — or to the sham of his existence and double life there, was about as remote as Elton John saying he was gay, that he only liked to dress that way for fun, and yes, the jewelry and mink capes did indeed come with the job.

Here he could finally be what he was without pretending to be something he wasn't. The masquerade was over.

Every day seemed like Halloween to Buddy, as gay men casually went about their business. And, no one was hiding the fact that they were gay. Within a week's time the towheaded Hoosier had seen, tasted, smelled and touched everything Boys' Town had to offer — from its tricks to its treats.

On the seventh day of his visit he found an overpriced single on Vista Grande, joined a health club, bought a new pair of black 501s from All American Boy and concluded his day by treating himself to the *table d'hôte* at a classy boulevard restaurant called Truffles. And, fate was smiling. He left Truffles, not only satiated but *employed*: waiting table in the main dining room.

By the time he'd progressed down the boulevard to sip an al-fresco Long Island Ice Tea at a bar called Rage, Indiana was becoming just another misty, water-colored memory.

He quietly considered his alternatives for the evening: A moustached blond that reminded him of his high school civics teacher; a smoldering moustached Latino in white painter pants and EAT THE WORM t-shirt; or a moustached bodybuilder with a diamond earring and a black panther tatooed to a bicep that looked like it belonged in a bowling bag.

Without preamble, he knew in his libidinal heart of hearts that there was no contest. The tattooed bicep and diamond-studded stud received a unanimous decision. Any last-minute qualms of his geographical relocation were swiftly laid to RIP.

He felt just like Dorothy in Oz.

# 5. Fool for Love

Writing is a solitary act. Like masturbation it is usually done alone. Unlike Love it rarely travels in pairs. Scout knew this because he was on intimate terms with all three; assiduous in his attention to the first two, and usually at the short end of the stick with the third. Emily Dickinson was right: "That love is all there is, is all we know of love." Scout took this as the gospel truth.

He was the Chuck Yeager of matters of the heart, flying without wings or safety net where lesser hearts feared to tread, never giving up. Hurdling Love's obstacle course — the decathlon of the heart — until he was blue in the face.

Compiling a list of past lovers, and its implications, his face looked like a disaster victim on the evening news whose house had relocated via a flood or tornado or an unexpected act of God. Sometimes he thought Love was purely mythical, that it was all done with mirrors; still he never gave up. The list confirmed it:

ANTONIO C.
ANGELO G.
MAXIMILLIAN T.
NOAH J.

Love was nonnegotiable. He wondered if Jesse Y. would be next. He had to admit, his track record was on a par with Lana Turner's. Four lovers in eight years. It was down to decimals.

He dragged on his cigarette.

The names and faces change, but the scenario, come the last reel, remains the same: boy meets boy, boy gets boy, boy loses boy; kisses, tears, fadeout. Was Nash really right? That we live in times of disposable *everything*. A society of consume and discard, including lovers.

Thirty birthdays had passed him by. It was time to either thaw out or freeze.

"Plotting another novel?" Nash asked.

Scout turned to him, wadding up the list, then threw it into a wicker basket beside the desk he had rescued from the local Goodwill. Nash was in his pre-work uniform: gym shorts and a dumbbell in each fist. The living room mirror he was standing in front of clearly reflected what was without a doubt the flesh of the typical gay man's fantasy — his housemate looked like a Tom of Finland original.

"Do you have to do *that* in here? Christ, the whole house is going to smell like the West Hollywood Athletic Club."

Nash glared at him. It was a look he usually reserved for inebriated queens suffering from a temporary loss of decorum in Truffles's main bar where he worked. Slowly, he lowered his muscular arms. "How in the hell would you know," he replied snidely. "You're hardly ever there any more. I take it some people find love handles attractive!"

"Yeah, well not everyone wants to look like fucking Conan the Barvarian!"

"That's *barbarian*, stupid — and everyone I know does!"

"Gays are such extremists."

The dumbbells clanked to the floor. "Hey, don't bark at me. You've had three dates with this carpenter in less than a week. If this is love, I'll take mine rare."

Scout whimpered like a puppy.

Nash recognized the symptoms and rolled his eyes. "I thought love was supposed to give you that rosy glow that you're always writing about."

"That's pregnancy — and I'm not always writing about it."

"Hey, I know what I'm talking about. That last book you wrote, *Glazed Fruit,* wasn't exactly a comedy. You haven't acted this way since Noah, may he rest in peace."

Nash was right. Since he had started seeing Jesse, butterflies of haiku-intensity had ambushed the inner sanctum of his solar plexus on glittered, Bob Mackie wings. "I have been on the rag, huh?"

"Does a mule have an ass? Is a frog's ass watertight?"

"All right, I get the picture."

Nash scratched the mounds of his spectacular pecs; pecs that caused customers at Truffles's main bar to drool like Pavlov's dog. "I don't think you do. I think you're in love."

"I have been craving chocolate."

Nash looked up, palms and fingers pressed together steeple-like in mock-prayer. His voice was a husky basso. "Help me make it through this one, Lord."

Scout laughed. "Am I *that* bad?"

"Worse! Some guys hear bells — you hear the 1812 Overture in stereophonic sound. When love hits you, it's like a 6.5 on the Richter scale. It doesn't happen often, but when it does, it's time to circle the wagons."

Nash was right. Scout had to hear the 1812, complete with cannons. If he didn't, what was the point? It had to be the real McCoy or nothing. No fillers; no substitutes. Some people could get by on no-strings-attached sex, but he wasn't one of them. Sex without love was unimaginable to him, which definitely put him in the minority in Boys' Town. It also explained why he loved so infrequently. Why the intervals between loving a man grew longer and longer. Love took so much out of him; trusting and loving one person, trying to make love root and grow without putting in a change of address every time a foible raised its nasty little head. It was an adult game, but sometimes the price paid was more than the quality of the goods received.

Nash strained under the weights. "So, what are you two love-birds up to this evening?"

"A quiet night at home with the kid. Family stuff. I'm going to rent some movies."

Nash grinned as the veins in his arms grew erections. "Movies? I didn't know Al Parker made family films."

# 6. Everybody is a Star

"Another bottle of Dom Perignon," Buddy gasped.

Six weeks before coming to Truffles, he wouldn't have known what Dom Perignon was, much less how to pronounce it; tonight it rolled off his tongue like Ripple.

Nash grinned from behind the bar. The freckled-faced young waiter amused him. Because of his down-home innocence and homogenized good looks, they had become good friends. West Hollywood was known for making meals out of fresh young things like Buddy, so Nash took it upon himself to look out for the waiter. He and Scout frequently had him over for dinner, which considering Scout's cooking, would test the friendship of anyone.

Shortly after moving to Boys' Town, Buddy had developed what Nash jokingly referred to as CSP: Celebrity Sensory Perception. Whenever a celebrity was near, Buddy cackled with excitement. He was a fan of just about everyone. Especially Cher. He still nursed a grudge against Linda Hunt for beating Cher out of the best supporting actress Oscar. "Let's be real," he'd said. "Linda Hunt is an excellent actress, but can you imagine her in a Bob Mackie gown? *Pulease*! I hear she buys all her clothes off the rack — the Barbie Collection!"

Tonight, he looked like the goose that laid the golden egg.

"Who is it?" Nash asked, although he already knew. Strategic eye contact had been made as the man and his entourage passed through the bar en route to the restaurant.

"Dan Carlton!" Buddy was aghast. "Can you believe it? And he's at my station, too. He's even better looking in person than he is on the four o'clock news."

"Is that so?"

"Dammit! I knew I shouldn't have skipped my workout at the gym today. I wonder if he's into scrawny vanilla?"

"There's only one way to find out."

"Do you really think he's *gay*? I mean, they're both with women, but if that other guy is straight, then I'm Annette Funicello for Skippy!"

"That's the rumor," Nash shrugged, placing the expensive champagne on the waiter's cork-lined tray. "I doubt if he wandered in here by mistake."

Buddy didn't hear the last part. He propelled himself through the crowded bar like an autograph hound, hot on the heels of a four o'clock anchorman — living proof that the best thing about being from Indiana was that just about everyone was a star of some sort.

Mike Mentzer could have spit the guy out. The resemblance was uncanny, down to the moustache and Incredible Hulk physique. He was dressed in a gray GOLD'S GYM tank top, which flatteringly showcased the impressive bulk of a torso that suggested to observers that Michelanglo did indeed study at the Gold's Gym School of Art, and ultra-tight, spray-on 501's that produced an identically flattering effect on the curves of his lower extremeties.

Leaning against the bar in a drunken sing-along with the latest Diana Ross chartbuster, Buddy eyed him suspiciously before motioning Nash over.

"DRQ!" he sniffed, glancing toward the mountain of muscle singing in a high, incongruous falsetto.

"Huh?" Nash followed the path of Buddy's innocent baby blues.

"DRQ — Diana Ross Queen!" Then, clandestinely, he stuffed a tightly folded note into the bartender's hand.

Without skipping a beat, Nash slipped it into the hip pocket of his jeans. He had the kind of face and physique that incited notes and hurriedly scribbled telephone numbers. "Who's it from?"

Buddy's eyes looked like klieg lights. "The Emmy-winning Dan Carlton," he whispered, as if anyone could hear above the echo chamber din of La Ross and her lone Supreme.

"How do you know it's for me?" Nash glanced toward the other bartenders.

"Because you're the only one with black hair and a moustache in a tank top that say's 'Let's Fuck' in Japanese!"

"How'd you know that? The Japanese, I mean."

Buddy's eyebrows darted to his hairline like an amateur

sleuth. "Because I bought one just like it, although the sales clerk assured me it was one of a kind. I should've known the bitch was lying — he had a low forehead and really beady eyes."

Nash grinned the grin of a man who is never without a date on the weekend. "Dan Carlton, huh?"

"Yeah. I think it was your hairy Mt. Fuji pecs that did it. I never had a chance," he said ruefully, surveying the flat pancake plane of his white Calvin Klein shirt. "I'm going to have to switch to steroids."

"You do that and your pecker will fall off."

Buddy blushed. "Well, if he doesn't autograph a menu for me, I'm switching to Marcia Brandewyn on Channel 11."

"Did you read the note?"

"Hey, I know I'm queer, but do I look like J. Edgar Hoover? Give me a break, Nash."

"Okay.' Leaning across the bar, Nash gave the waiter's derriere a congratulatory pat for a job well done; ball player to ball player as it were.

Sometime past midnight, Nash slipped into the employee's bathroom behind the kitchen. Locking the door behind him, he extracted the note from his hip pocket and unfolded it. A crisp one hundred dollar bill wafted to the floor like a new fallen leaf. Was this guy for real? Shaking his head incredulously, he grabbed the bill from the floor, then read the note:

VOULEZ VOUS COUCHER AVEC MOI?
CIAO — D. C.

Nash snorted. "What an asshole. A polyglot, too."

He tore the note in two and bull's-eyed it into the toilet and flushed. "Ciao — D. C."

Declining two rendezvous at two different after-hour bars, breakfast at the Yukon, coffee at the French Quarter, and a singularly blatant, "Wanna fuck?" Nash slipped out Truffles's back door and into the alley. Standing in the darkness, a cigarette propped between petulant lips, he waited like a protagonist in a Joe Gage porno film.

In the distance, headlights flicked on and steel-belted radials crunched over loose gravel. A smokey-green Mercedes coupe coasted slowly to his feet. An electric window lowered. There in the darkness was a smile that only a crocodile could approximate.

Cool was Nash's vocation. Taking a final drag from his cigarette, he brought his hand down, flipping the butt across the alley. He lowered his head to the window. "*Comment ça va?*"

Dan Carlton's smile was caught with its pants down around its ankles. "Huh?" He bluffed it. "Climb in."

Nash had every intention of telling the arrogant anchorman exactly where to go, how to get there and precisely what to do with his money. Instead, he took one look at the unearthly green eyes and climbed in beside him.

Sparks flew. It was either a case of *so many men and so little time* or Dan Carlton's turbo charisma. Whatever it was, both men felt its kinetic charge jolt their libidos.

The anchorman had his act down pat as he pulled the brawny bartender to his lips. He was a character actor of arrogance.

"Live around here?"

Nash felt like a piece of meat, which didn't particularly faze him since he was used to dealing on that level, but he didn't like not having the upper hand.

"Come on, man. I know you want it as much as I do!"

Nash couldn't argue with that point. "Let's go."

The anchorman smiled suggestively. He knew that he had Nash, and the only thing left was to reel him in.

Nash caught a glimmer of light across the bridge of perfectly capped white teeth. Dan Carlton shifted to drive and floored it. Being a celebrity had its advantages. Fans rarely said no to S & M: Sex and Money.

# 7. The Family Way

Jesse was in the back yard building a jungle gym for his son when Scout arrived carrying a black plastic bag. *Video West* was slashed across the front in hot, vibrating purple.

Jesse's face lit up like a Christmas tree; like a small boy who'd gotten everything Santa had promised. "Hey, handsome. I'll be right with you."

Scout smiled, settling on the grass beside the carpenter, who was dressed in a soft flannel shirt, unbuttoned to the pectorals and rolled up at the sleeves. His faded Levis were torn at the knee and faded everywhere else from wear. On Jesse they looked like authentic work clothes, not the national gay attire.

Suddenly, from behind, a pair of tiny hands strained to cover his eyes. A crescendo of childish laughter followed. Then, a husky little voice. "Guess who?"

Scout acted surprised. "Is it . . . Michael Jackson?"

"Nooo," Jackson squealed.

"Is it . . . Truman Capote?"

"Noooooo!"

"Then, it's Quentin Crisp?"

"Nooo." Jackson's giggle gurgled uncontrollably from his throat. "It's me! It's me!" he giggled, racing around to Scout's face, convinced that he'd fooled him. "Hey, Pop, Scout didn't know it was me!"

Snuggled inside a *Star Wars* sleeping bag, inches from the TV screen, the sandman had dusted Jackson off before Dumbo made his first solo flight; before the circus jerks overpowered a screaming Mrs. Jumbo, separating her from her flop-eared offspring. (She didn't even have time to pack her trunk).

Maizie (Mazola Stills — Jesse's black housekeeper and surrogate mother to Jackson) wandered in from the kitchen, drying her hands on a faded calico bib apron. Her eyes were fixed on Scout. "What's wrong with him?"

Jesse tried not to laugh. Tears were streaming down Scout's cheeks. He winked at Maizie. "Poor Dumbo."

She shook her head. Scout obviously identified.

"Want me to drive you home?"

"No, I'll walk. Maybe I can burn off some of those calories from the ice cream." She glanced at Scout, who was polishing off a container of Rum Raisin Haagen-Dazs. "If he doesn't stop feeding his face, he'll be as big as I am."

"You're not fat, Maizie," Jesse laughed. "You've just got big bones." And she did, too. She was a handsome black woman of indeterminable age, with high Cherokee cheekbones and curly salt-and-pepper hair.

"Well, I'll see you tomorrow," she said, removing her apron.

"Bye, girl." Scout didn't take his eyes from the TV screen.

"Now, you two be good and don't do anything I wouldn't do."

"That doesn't leave much," Jesse winked, referring to her former four husbands. She had buried them all, and Jesse swore she had worn them out.

Scout flashed her a look of mock-despair. "If you're going, girl, I wish you'd go." He wiped his eyes. "I'm trying to watch Dumbo!"

She shook her head. "If that don't beat all — a grown man crying over a midget pachyderm."

"Go home, Maizie."

She reached over and gave Scout's head a good thump.

"You want me to leave, but it doesn't have a damn thing to do with Dumbo!"

That caught him off guard. Jesse gave his shoulder a reassuring squeeze, then walked Maizie to the front door.

Scout licked his spoon clean, then flicked off the TV. He let out a long sigh. "How did Disney get away with that anthropomorphic bullshit? Jesus, it could tear a kid's heart out. It's worse than Bette Davis in *Dark Victory!*"

Jesse returned, lifting Jackson over his shoulder. "Not to mention grown men. I'll put him to bed and be right back."

When he came into the living room, he was stripped down to his underwear. This time when Scout sighed, it wasn't for Dumbo.

# 8. Afternoon Delight

Among other things, Dan Carlton had an ego of gargantuan proportions.

Nash gave him four stars between the sheets, but out of bed he was just another man wrestling with internal demons.

"This isn't the McCarthy era," he said, leaning across the bed for a post-coital cigarette. "We're not *communists* for christssakes! And, I seriously doubt if you're the only gay anchorman on the air waves."

Dan Carlton didn't want to discuss it. The subject Nash insisted on rehashing was like a broken record to him, and he was sick of hearing it. Jumping out of bed, he made for the solitude of the bathroom shower.

Nash studied the retreating musculature, the broad shoulders and slim hips, with the patient eyes of a true connoisseur. The former college quarterback was Grade A Choice. Nash knew his beef, but he didn't know that he had learned more about the anchorman than any of the desultory affairs that had preceded him. In the few weeks that they had been seeing each other, an added ingredient had manifested in their relationship that kept them both on guard.

After snubbing his cigarette in the ashtray beside the bed, he strolled casually into the bathroom. "Hey, can you hear me in there?"

"I don't want to discuss it," Dan shouted.

"Jesus, you sound just like Scout. He may not be your typical gay man, but he isn't ashamed of being *ho-mo-sex-u-al*."

The word made Dan Carlton cringe. "Listen," he said, poking his head from behind the shower curtain, "don't fuck this up. We've got a good thing going here, so do us both a favor and shut up!"

Nash waited for the shower to shut off. "You call this a good thing?"

He glared at him as he stepped from the shower. "Yes, I do."

"Oh," Nash continued, following him into the bedroom, "is that why you're in such a goddamn hurry to get out of here? Afraid Scout might come home and see us like this? Two grown men. Naked!"

Dan toweled off, then darted for his clothes.

"You want to play heterosexual? Okay. Heterosexual men have male friends, too."

"Not male friends with tattoos and a diamond earring."

"Hey, for all anyone knows, I might have gotten this tattoo in the service."

"The Marines, no doubt."

"Well, it sure as hell wasn't the WACs! Is it my fault Uncle Sam is homophobic?"

Dan buttoned his shirt. "Listen, I told you I have a condo in Hawaii. We can go there any time you want. We can do things there together if we're discreet."

"*Discreet!* Why do we have to fly across a fucking ocean to do things together?"

"Because that's the way it is." He pulled on his Italian sport coat, and took a small box from the pocket.

"What's that?"

"Open it." Except for his father, it was the first time he'd ever given another man a present.

Inside was a 24K gold cobra chain.

"It's nice," Nash deadpanned, "but I was hoping for a *Longine*."

"Smartass!"

"What brought this on?"

"For giving me back my money that first night. I guess I had you figured all wrong."

"I almost flushed it down the john."

"And . . . for being a nice guy."

"Thanks."

Dan was beginning to feel awkward.. Sex was one thing; his emotions another. "Well, I'd better get going."

"Hey," Nash yelled, before Dan managed a clean getaway. "Think about what I said. About going to the Gay Pride Parade with me. Maybe we could get you a blonde wig and disguise you as Jane Pauley!"

"Guess who I just saw?" Scout set two Safeway bags on the kitchen counter.

"Jimmy Hoffa?"

"No, that news guy — Dean Carter."

Nash slapped his forehead. "It's *Dan*, not Dean. And, it's *Carlton*, not Carter."

"Yeah, that's the one. Something must be going on in the neighborhood. He was running up the street."

"Something is going on in the neighborhood. He was just here."

"In tne house?"

"In my bedroom to be exact."

Scout was incredulous. He lifted a Van de Kamp's Swiss Chocolate Chip Cake from one of the bags and placed it on the new butcher block Jesse had made for them. "In your bedroom? What the hell is going on?"

Nash could see the light click on above Scout's head.

"You mean — you and Dean..."

"*Dan*, damnit!"

"Yeah, yeah, but I thought he was straight."

"If he is, he's got a funny way of showing it."

"No! You two ... are..."

"You can say it. We're all adults here."

"No! This is a joke, right?"

Nash examined his cuticles. "I can't recall that anyone was laughing."

Scout's eyes looked like saucers. "Jeeze. I don't think you've ever *done it* with a celebrity before — except for Paulo, but he wasn't actually a celebrity." He pulled a chair from the kitchen table and sat down. "Well, tell me all about it. How'd all this happen?"

Nash stared at him. "I'd rather not discuss it."

# 9. Seeing Stars

It was a moon of paradoxes. A moon of yin; a moon of yang. It was a moon of sonnets and love songs and chilling mysteries and unsolved crimes. It was a moon with an ace up its sleeve and a bag of tricks that'd make Doug Henning envious. It could exert unseen forces over ocean tides and transmute ordinary people into howling werewolves and still keep a poker face. It was a vampire's sun. A golf course for astronauts. It was that *extra* something in a voodoo curse. Yet, it was nothing more than a benign smile hovering above the earth like a toddlers' nursery rhyme.

Tonight, high above Boys' Town, its opalescent mantle waxed cool and calm, with champagne luminosity, like a paper moon in a Fred and Ginger musical; its jeweled brilliance clung to the neck of an indigo sky like a rare lunar pearl. Waiting for a little night music, a little romance, a little mayhem.

Buddy, not really wanting to carouse, but unable to disengage himself from the cruise control state he'd been in since his arrival, operated on automatic pilot as he got ready for another night on the town.

He washed his face with Laszlo. Toned with Clinique. Wreathed himself in *Kouros*. Moussed, styled, blowed and bent his hair into shape. Slipped into a new Takis Greek shirt from International Male. Into a pair of tight 501s, and hooked his keys on the appropriate side of his belt. All within three-quarters of an hour. The night was about to begin. He checked the results in the bathroom mirror and it was All Systems Go.

But where was he going?

He scanned the local bar guide for ideas while toking from the last of his home-grown Hoosier grass:

A Tan Line Contest at the Eagle.

A Leathermen's Beer Bust at Greg's Blue Dot.

An Equinox Dance at Rage.

A Battle of the Cocks Contest, which boggled his mind, at The Corral Club.

An All Male Review at Woody's.

Videos at Revolver.

MotherLode and the *creme de la creme* of Boys' Town.

He sighed in exasperation.

Finally, there was Le Jazz Hot at the Four Star. That was within walking distance. Plus, it held the added attraction of Max, a sexy, slim-hipped Mexican dancer who set Buddy's heart pounding like castanets. He crossed his fingers. After mooning over the dancer for weeks, maybe tonight was the night he would summon up the courage to ask Max for a date. There was a rumor that he was hot for blonds.

He stepped in dog shit as he left the apartment and had to go back and change his shoes. It never occurred to him that the misfortunate step might be a portent of the things to come that evening.

When he finally reached the boulevard, he had shaken a stirring that told him to stay at home for the evening and relax.

Bustling with activity, the boulevard was filled with men in every conceivable shape and size, though muscles definitely seemed *de rigueur*. Muscles, like Gucci and Vuitton, had become the new gay status symbol and everyone had them or was in the process of obtaining them. He hesitated a moment and took a deep breath. There sure wasn't anything like it in Indiana.

Eros was in the air as he skipped past the alfresco diners at the Greenery, trying to fake himself into another night at the bars. A few feet ahead of him, Scout was coming out of Haagen-Dazs. He quickened his pace and caught up with him.

"Scout!"

"Hey, what's cookin', good-lookin'?" Scout wiped the traces of White Chocolate from his moustache. "Out prowlin' again, huh?"

Buddy flushed embarrassingly.

Scout turned to his companion. "Jesse, this is Buddy. He works at Truffles with Nash."

Jesse extended a tanned, snaked-veined forearm. "I've heard a lot about you, Buddy. Nice to meet you."

"Same here," he grinned, shaking the firm hand. He quickly surveyed Scout's lover, concluding that Scout had found *the* man at the end of the rainbow. "So, what are you guys up to tonight?"

"I had this unnatural craving for ice cream," Scout said guiltily. "I don't know what's wrong with me. I can't seem to stop eating."

It was obvious to Buddy. It was Love. Jesse was tanned and handsome and without affectation. Definitely a man secure with his masculinity — he wasn't even showing a basket!

"He's got a sweet tooth like Shelley Winters," Jesse grinned, draping his hand over Scout's shoulder.

Buddy shifted on his heels. The mana between them could have given Edison a run for its money.

"Hey, why don't you skip the bars and come home with us," Scout suggested. "Nash is there. We're going to watch *The Boys in the Band* on TV."

Buddy hedged. "Maybe later. I'm going to see Le Jazz Hot at the Four Star."

"Le Jazz Hot or Le Jazz' Max?" Scout needled. "Shoot, Bud, ask him out. Max is a fool if he says no."

"Go for the gusto *,*" Jesse coaxed.

Scout patted him on the shoulder. "Go get 'em Romeo, but if you change your mind, you know where to find us."

"Okay," He waved to them as they turned up a dark street, a full moon beckoning high above their heads.

He missed the first show.

Suddenly, the mood to party escaped him, disappearing as fleetingly as it had arrived. He quickly surveyed the bar. Only the hardcore were out tonight.

As he was about to leave, a man on a stool close to where he was standing called to him from the semi-darkness. "Hey, kid!"

Buddy smiled weakly. The man was fifty if he was a day, in a black leather vest, no shirt and strategically torn Levis. A belly the size of a beer barrel hung over the edge of a Harley-Davidson belt buckle like a painting by Salvador Dali. The man was licking his lips obscenely. Buddy felt like a chicken leg in a Colonel Sanders commercial.

"I was just leaving," he said sheepishly.

The man cupped his crotch. "Don't leave, kid. I bet I can tell you your fortune if you sit on my face!"

Laughter echoed behind him as he beat a path out the door. Safely on the sidewalk, he headed in the direction of Nash and Scout's house.

He turned off the boulevard on to Hilldale, but it wasn't until he reached the alley behind the Bank of America that he noticed them: three beer-guzzling punks, the oldest no more than seventeen.

Trouble mingled in the air like static electricity. He shouldn't have broken stride, but they had caught him off guard. He decided to go for it, and started past them.

"Hey, sissy! Wanna suck my dick?"

He cringed but kept going, looking directly ahead. Suddenly a beer bottle smashed at his feet. Don't look back, he told himself. *Don't* look back. He froze and looked back. They were already coming toward him.

"Hey, faggot, I got something for you," one laughed obnoxiously. "It's a big muthafucker, too!"

His pals laughed as if he was the Sakharov of *bon mots*.

Buddy swallowed hard. Adrenaline raced through his veins

like a speedballed thoroughbred at Santa Anita. A clammy sweat broke out across his forehead and upper lip. He wanted to run, but his feet seemed to be cemented to the sidewalk.

One of them pushed his shoulder. "Hey, cocksucker, my friend here asked you a question."

"I don't want any trouble, fellas," he said meekly, wondering if they could smell his fear. He had read that animals could do that, and these guys looked like animals.

"This litter peckerhead doesn't want any trouble, guys."

"Bash the fag."

One of them with a greasy punk hairdo and a blood-dripping dagger tattooed to his shoulder moved in closer. Snarling teeth pushed their way into Buddy's face. They looked subhuman. "We're gonna kill your cocksuckin' ass, faggot."

It was like a bad dream. Buddy watched helplessly as they overpowered him.

An elbow smashed into his profile, cracking hard against his nose. A fist of knuckles exploded against his eye. Within seconds, they were on him like mad, eviscerating dogs.

He was already falling when a beer bottle rose high above his head. In one swift swoop it cracked against his skull with a dull, resounding thud. A galaxy of stars rotated around his head like tiny, blinking zircons.

"Fuckin' cocksucker!" echoed in his ears.

His eyes rolled involuntarily into their sockets. His body surrendered like an abandoned marionette, collasping in a heap on the coarse cement. Blood surged from a deep crack in his skull. Then he saw it . . .

An albescent glow appeared from above. *One universal smile it seem'd of all things; Joy past compare; gladness unutterable; Imperishable life of peace and love; Exhaustless . . . unmeasured bliss.* Dante written in preternatural light, like the milky insides of an exquisite pearl.

A piercing scream slashed the darkness like the hard, cold steel of a switchblade. In the distance, a black woman was racing down Hilldale toward the assailing punks.

The ferocity of her second scream brought porch lights and people from the boulevard.

She was on them like white on rice. Bashing, clawing and

biting anything she could get her hands on. Her purse was like David's sling, cracking between the eyes of one of the boys like a leather boulder. "Shit!" he screamed. They quickly knocked her to the ground, but not before she connected with a fistful of greasy hair, yanking it out by the roots.

As they fled, she bent over the inert figure, tears welling in her dark eyes. "Sweet Jesus, what have they done to you?"

A crowd quickly gathered, among them a bartender from Truffles. He recognized the victim immediately.

"Someone call an ambulance!" a voice screamed.

The bartender was out of breath when he reached their house. Jesse and Nash were on the sofa, howling over Scout's latest article on feminine protection: "Concrete: The Single Woman's Guide to Burglar-Proofing the Home." Scout was contently nibbling on a piece of fried chicken left over from dinner when the bartender began pounding wildly on their front door. It sounded like an earthquake.

"Jesus fucking Christ!" Scout gasped, practically inhaling a chicken leg as Jesse and Nash raced to the door.

"He's in the hospital," the bartender said, with a sharp intake of air. "I think . . . he might . . . be dead."

"What?" Nash shouted. "Who's dead?"

"Buddy! Buddy Dove!"

# 10. Where's the Beef?

An impromtu forum was underway in the main dining room at Truffles.

"We've got to do something about this," Nash shouted, hammering his fist against a table like a gavel. "We have to protect our own!"

"Like what?" a bartender from MotherLode asked.

"Maybe we could form a posse and go after the sonsofbitches. Maybe the police will join forces with the gay community."

"Fuck the police!" a gravelly voice yelled.

"I have!" someone shot back.

"I bet tnere was an entire fleet of them down at Winchell's Donuts when it happened," a waiter snapped. "They're never around when you need them, but they're right on time when you don't."

"Amen!" someone testified.

"I like Nash's idea. Why don't we form a posse? Like a local vigilante group to patrol the area."

Someone spoke up in back. "We could go around to all the gyms and put up recruiting posters."

"And the bars, too," another voice added. "My lover's a commercial artist. I bet he'd design the poster."

"Something in *art deco*," an aesthetically-minded man yelled.

"The Gay Pride Parade is coming up," Nash injected. "I think we should get a float together. Gays from all over will see it then."

"Right on!"

Random fists shot up in solidarity.

"We could wear uniforms, too," a bartender named Louis suggested.

Nash frowned. "Hey, we're not fascists!"

"Jeans and Lacostes are *fascist?*"

"Yeah," a carpenter friend of Louis's shouted. "*Pink* Lacostes — at least no one will have to buy one."

"All right!" another bartender yelled. "*Pink Power!* I bet the local news would carry it, too. What do you think, Nash?"

Nash didn't have a chance to reply. A moustached man with cantaloupe-sized biceps stood up, commanding the floor like a huge, gay Goliath. He looked like he could bench press a house. "I think we *should* form a gay militia. Hell, most of us are built like Marines, we might as well start acting like them. I say, *Let's Kick Ass!!*"

A thunderous roar of approval shook Truffles's dining room. Presently, everyone was on their feet. A chant enveloped the room: "Pink Power! Pink Power! Pink Power!"

Dan Carlton was not amused.

"Are you nuts?" He shot Nash an acerbic look. "I can't get involved with this."

Nash removed his lips from the anchor's nipple, catching a hair between his teeth.

"Ouch! Damnit!"

"What a pussy!" He inspected the hair as if it were a rare flower he might want to press between the pages of a book for posterity. "Why the hell not?"

"I am *not* participating or lending my support to that damn Gay Pride Parade! Period!"

"Goddamnit, I'm not asking you to wear a prom gown and wave from a float." Now he was riled. "Just *be there*! For once show where your true sympathies are for christssakes. Lots of celebrities support gay causes, if for nothing else than the free publicity."

"You know damn well that I don't want *that* kind of publicity." Except for his career, the bartender filled him with an all-consuming passion he had never experienced before. If Nash were a ride at Disneyland, he'd be an *E* ticket.

Nash was in no mood to fuck with a man who was gay but pretended ninety-five percent of the time that he wasn't.

"Come back to bed, damnit."

Nash stared at him long and hard, then started pulling on his jeans. "You know, Al Parker once said, 'Everyone is responsible for their own orgasm.'"

"And, what's that suppose to mean?"

Nash buttoned his shirt. "It means, God gave you two hands — use them!"

# 11. Open House

Buddy looked like a cornucopia on which the Jolly Green Giant had danced a cha-cha. His lips looked like rotten pomegranates. Where his eyes used to be were two badly bruised grapes. His head resembled a coconut with a shaved, punk hairdo. He was a mess.

Nash cringed. "Jeeeesssuuusss! Do you always look like this in the morning, Bud?" He handed his friend a bouquet of roses and baby's breath. "Just kidding, Bud."

"Here," Scout grinned, kicking Nash's shin as he placed a stack of magazines on the hospital bed. *"Blueboy, Torso, In Touch —* all the essential periodicals for the discerning gay shut-in. The interview I did with Rita Mae Brown is in there, too. Maybe you can get one of those cute interns to read it to you."

Maizie eyed them, dying to peek at the pictures. "Here, sugar. Sweets for the sweet. Homemade fudge."

"This is from Jackson," Jesse said brightly, propping an over-stuffed Garfield cat under Buddy's arm. "He insisted that you have it to keep you company."

Gumdrop tears welled in Buddy's black and blue eyes.

"Now, don't cry," Maizie smiled, patting his arm. "The boys got a real nice surprise for you."

"Yeah, Bud," Nash winked, "perk up. We've got a little floor show for you." He motioned toward the door with his hand. "The *pièce de résistance!*"

On cue, the waiters and bartenders from Truffles filed in one by one, carrying a huge horseshoe of rainbow-colored flowers. A pink satin sash declared: BEING SICK IS A DRAG — GET WELL SOON!

Then, popping out from behind the line, a waiter in white nurse drag scurried around the room, holding an enema bag of strawberry margaritas at arm's length.

Maizie howled.

The nurse skipped around the room, eyeing everyone suspiciously. "I heard one of ya'll was sick around here," she articulated, in perfect Bette Midler fashion, "but don't none of ya'll look too sick to me." Then, with a deft swoop of her arm, she parted the sea of male bodies. She pointed an accusing finger toward the hospital bed. " 'Cept for you, honey — you look like ssshhiiittt!"

Maizie fell out laughing, practically knocking Buddy out of bed.

She then flipped a strand of her blonde Marilyn Monroe wig from her shoulder, reached inside her uniform and produced a bevy of plastic cocktail glasses from her bosom, quickly deflating her breasts. She served Buddy first, then wiggled her padded hips over to the old gentleman peeking from behind a curtain in the next bed.

"Are you my nurse?" he asked benignly.

"Honey, I'm *everybody's* nurse!" She handed him a cocktail. "Drink this, hon — it's good for what ails ya!"

Everyone laughed as Mr. Peralez joined in the fun.

Buddy couldn't tell if his lips were working, but his heart was smiling shoulder to shoulder.

Maizie was next, and the nurse nudged her as she handed her a drink, motioning towards Buddy. "Shit, girl, he's starting to look better already!"

# 12. Two Tons of Fun

Comfortably reposed against the upholstered headboard of Jesse's bed, Scout watched with unbridled glee as Joan Crawford put the screws to her sinister sibling, Veda.

"You should see this, Jesse," he said playfully, munching from a box of Fiddle Faddle.

Jesse was on the floor executing his nightly calisthenics.

"Shoot, this is better than *Dynasty!* The bitch fight of all time."

Jesse groaned from the floor where he was doing sit-ups.

"Get her, Joan," Scout rooted. "Throw the hussy out on the street where she belongs. Hit her with a pie!"

Veda was out on her ass, chanteusing it up in a seedy waterfront dive when Jesse finished his exercises and climbed into bed next to Scout.

Scout turned briefly from the TV and stared at his lover's muscularly lean torso. He did a quick survey of the delineated abdomen and broad, square shoulders. Then, just as quickly, his eyes detoured to his own body.

"What's wrong?" Jesse's hand was on the slight protrusion of Scout's belly.

"Look at me. I'm getting . . . *fat!*"

"You are not," he chuckled softly. "A little pudgy is all."

Scout was mortified. It was one thing to pass judgment on himself, it was another to have his lover confirm it. He could have cried. "I look like a sumo wrestler."

Jesse snorted. "You're exaggerating. Besides, I think it's kinda cute."

"*What?*"

He stroked the not-so-flat plane of Scout's stomach. "This little Buddha belly you're getting."

"*Buddha belly!*" He sprang from the bed, knocking an empty box of Fiddle Faddle to the floor. There was a full-length mirror behind Jesse's bedroom door, and he quickly composed himself before it.

Jesse laughed.

Scout wasn't so amused. "Look! I've got abominable abdominals. I'm a P.I.G. Hog!"

"You are not." Jesse got up and walked behind Scout, resting his chin on his lover's shoulder, speaking to the reflection in the mirror. "It's these boxer shorts you're wearing. There's enough room in there for the Gay Men's Marching Band."

"No, it's me." The verdict was out and Scout hung his head in shame. "I don't go to the gym anymore. Even Nash said so. Then I met you, and now Buddy. I'm a mess."

Jesse chuckled, slowly turning Scout around until they were face to face. "Hey, handsome," he whispered, lifting Scout's chin with his forefinger. "I'd love you if you weighed a ton."

"That's what they all say. When I'm tipping the scales at five hundred pounds, you'll be hotfooting it to Boys' Town, with a slim-hipped kid with a twenty-nine-inch waist."

"I will not!"

"I bet." He glanced back at the mirror, convinced he was only pounds away from becoming Shamu the whale.

"Come on," Jesse coaxed, leading him back to bed.

"Turn out the lights first!" He took a deep breath and sucked in his belly.

# 13. Sugar Blues

En route to the gym, Scout stopped by the hospital to give Buddy some moral support. His mama always said that a hospital was no place to get well.

"Want some candy?" Buddy passed a box of vanilla walnut fudge Maizie had brought by.

"No thanks. I'm trying to quit." He pushed the box back across the bed. "Well, Bud, you're looking much better. Nash and I were talking about having you live with us for a while. I don't know how you're fixed for money, but you're welcome to stay with us — rent free."

Coincidentally, Buddy had been thinking about that very thing all morning. Worrying about his lack of income. Contemplating a return to Indiana. Now, his friends had come to his rescue. Tears formed in his eyes.

Scout rolled his eyes. "Now, don't start bawling or you'll have me crying, too."

"I don't know what to say, Scout."

He pointed a finger to his moustached lips. "Read my lips: YES. Now, you say it."

The shut-in sniffled and smiled. "Yes."

The man was dressed in chinos and a floral-print tapered shirt, opened to the navel. A wisp of afternoon breeze caressed the fabric, revealing Ferrigno-size pecs that left Boys' Town motorists and pedestrians gaping at the mouth. They flexed seductively as a green Volvo, with an I'D RATHER BE READING JANE AUSTEN bumper sticker rounded the corner.

Scout got the red light.

There was a parking space in front of Unity Savings. If he threw it into reverse, he could nab it, run into Mrs. Field's Cookies, and be out before having to put a dime in the parking meter.

It was a mini-battle of conscience, with conscience doing a fast two-step around reason. Half a dozen cookies isn't going to hurt anyone, an inner voice urged. Go for it! Start your diet tomorrow.

The sugar monkey on Scout's back was turning into King Kong. He was like an addict needing another fix.

He glanced briefly at the man with the headlight pecs and pencil-thin waist. It was all the encouragement he needed. The light turned green and he floored it. The gym and a slimmer physique was only a few blocks down the boulevard.

# 14. Life in a Goldfish Bowl

Everyone seemed to be on the lookout for Mr. Right, although most were settling for a close facsimile.

It was a question of logistics, and the situation being what it was, somebody had to lose or settle for second best. Leftovers à la beau.

Statistically, there are two women for every man, and thirteen percent of the available men are gay, which doesn't make a lot of women happy, creating a slim-pickin's effect all around, and this was not taking into consideration the undisclosed percentage that neither sex would touch with a ten-foot pole.

It didn't take Woody Allen to calculate that bisexuals stood the best chance, come Saturday night, of not only getting a date, but of making that magical connection with Mr. Right. The Good, the Bad and the Ugly had to fend for themselves.

Then came the lucky. Nash, being a minority (male) within a minority (gay), had fluked out completely. He wasn't even looking for Mr. Right when the close facsimile of Dan Carlton appeared on the scene. And now that he had him, Nash wasn't entirely sure what to do with him. But then, that was always the way — the rich got richer, the poor got poorer, and the lucky got *laid!*

"Hey, listen to this," Nash said, reading aloud from a new gossip rag circulating in Boys' Town called *Hollywood Tattletales.* "'What macho TV sitcom star is giving head to his drug dealer? And was last seen perusing the leather department at Pleasure Chest? Our in-store spy told us the Mr. Macho TV Star modeled black chaps for a hunky black employee, exposing his famous cheeks for everyone present!!!'"

Dan looked up from the crossword puzzle he was working on.

"They should be sued."

"I wonder who it is?"

"Who cares?"

"I do for one." Nash turned his attention to the movie listings. "Hey, there's a Tuesday Weld film retrospective at the Nuart on Wednesday."

"Today's Monday."

"Then how about Chinese food?"

Dan glanced at him, then returned to his puzzle.

"No way." Nash answered himself. "Too many people in a restaurant. We might be seen together."

Dan frowned. "What's a seven-lettered word for guilty?"

Nash blew the answer to him like an aborigine with a poisoned dart. "*Suspect.* S-u-s..."

"I can spell it, smartass!"

"Jesus H. Christ, let's go out. This bedroom is starting to give me claustrophobia!"

"Why don't we send *out* for Chinese food?"

"Why don't we call up your girlfriends, then we can go *out* and no one will be *suspect!*"

"Give it a rest, Nash."

"Jesus!" Nash stood up and stretched his considerable muscles. "Then let's go over to Jesse's and visit Scout."

"I don't think Scout cares for me."

"He just thinks you're the Elephant Man."

"The what?"

"The Elephant Man — you know," he lowered his voice to a distorted plea, "I am ... a ... human being."

"What's that got to do with me?"

"Don't ask, okay?"

"No. Tell me." He put down his crossword puzzle.

"Forget it."

"Damnit, I want to know. Does Scout think I'm a freak, or what?"

Nash scratched his bare chest, found his Calvin's balled up at the end of the bed, and put them on. "He just thinks you're hiding behind a mask. That you're pretending to be something you're not. He's been that way ever since Harvey Milk was assassinated."

"What does Harvey Milk and the Elephant Man have to do with me? I suppose Scout would like me to come out on the news — Hey, everybody in TV land, I'm gay."

Nash stared at him. "It might improve your ratings."

"It might cost me my fucking job!"

"So, you're a hypocrite, what's new? This town is full of

hypocrites. Actors, singers — you name it. I understand. We all have our little secrets."

"Scout, too?"

"Scout, too. Anyway, it's no skin off my back. I'd just like to do something outside of this bedroom for a change."

Dan reached for him, pulling him to the bed. "Listen, I don't care what Scout thinks of me, I just want..."

Nash pulled away. "I know what you want, and you can get *that* anywhere."

"You want it, too," he replied smugly. "You were moaning for it a little while ago."

Nash matched his look of disgust, more for himself than for Dan's statement. He was a slave to sex, but that didn't make it any easier to digest. It didn't help to assuage the feeling that he was just one more sexual entree on the buffet of the anchorman's life. There had to be a way to convince Dan that there was life outside the bedroom; outside the closet; outside the fishbowl existence of a relationship based on the rectangular construction of a mattress. There was more to life than heating up designer sheets. Damn, he thought, I'm beginning to sound like Scout.

# 15. Cleaning House

There wasn't much in Buddy's apartment to pack; an AM/FM clock-radio, a plastic mustard-colored Parson's table, a blow-dryer, two toothbrushes, some clothes, and the remains of a pepperoni and fungus pizza.

It reminded Scout of his college days at Brown, when he and Nash shared a funky two-room apartment in the heart of Providence, existing on Velveeta cheese sandwiches and care packages from home. When *less is more* was not an axiom of interior design, but a cold fact of matriculating existence.

He discovered a stack of letters under Buddy's mattress, and loaded them and everything else into the trunk of the Volvo, then headed for an aerobics class at the gym to sweat and stretch and gyrate his *more* into *less*.

The instructor at the gym was militant. A drill sergeant in pink and purple tights, with a fluffy bouffant of sun-streaked blonde hair that bounded like a trampoline.

"Come on people," she shouted above the pounding disco beat blaring from unseen speakers. "Let's move it! Let's firm up those flabby buttocks, those droopy thighs, those inner-tube waistlines. Move it . . . Go for the burn! Go for the burn!"

Fuck you, Scout thought, gasping for breath, kicking his legs in the air while slapping his hands beneath them. This bitch had obviously been watching too many Jane Fonda videos.

"Jumping jacks," she yelled. "Get those hands high above your heads. Stretch your legs. Take it to the max!"

Scout wanted to take it out the door to the nearest Fat Burger, yet he strained to kick higher; to twist harder; to go for *the burn.*

The people around him actually had smiles on their faces as they kicked and slapped and twisted, like blind fanatics in some weird religious cult, their bodies oil slicks of sweat. The bouncing blonde was their heroic leader, their guru to the perfect, fat-free body. Fat was their sin and a god-like body, rippling with taut musculature, was their ultimate goal, their nirvana. He wanted to rip out their throats.

His heart kicked into overdrive, beating inside his chest like a mechanical drum set at warp speed.

The gym instructor winked at him. "All right, now. *Double time!"*

When he returned home from the physical torture of the gym, swearing never to eat another Twinkie, something struck him as not quite right. He could feel it in the air the way an animal senses an approaching earthquake.

Something is wrong with this picture, he thought as an SOS flashed through the network of his brain cells, the only part of his body not limp with fatigue. A mottled tom cat poked its head from behind the back door, cased the yard, then scurried across the lawn into the shrubbery.

Wait a second, he thought, getting out of the car — we don't have a cat!

Tiptoeing to the back door, he listened for any signs of movement inside the house. It was quieter than a Helen Reddy concert.

His heart was in his throat as he entered.

The kitchen looked the same. The dining room looked the same. The living room...

"Sonofabitch!" His desk had been thoroughly ransacked. His typewriter was gone. The bookshelves had been pillaged, and books were thrown pellmell about the room. His eyes flew to where his antique French crystal Clichy paperweight should have been sitting. "Goddamnit!" he snapped.

The TVs in both bedrooms were gone. So were the VCRs, the stereos, tape decks and alarm clocks.

Rushing back to the living room to call the police, he suddenly wanted to scream — the telephone had been stolen, too.

# 16. Sleuth

Nash helped Scout with the inventory.

"Will you relax. The insurance will take care of everything. We're covered." His housemate was one seething queer.

"It won't replace my Clichy paperweight that Noah bought me in Europe that summer. Or my typewriter. *Sentiment* is priceless!"

Nash rolled his eyes. "Talk about cheap sentiment — you said yourself that that typewriter should have been put out of its misery long ago."

"You callous, musclebound sonofabitch! You used that typewriter to get through college. I *wrote* my first novel on it. It's part of our lives."

"That piece of junk? I hated it. The f-f-fucking *f* was always sticking. You couldn't get twenty cents for it at a flea market for the blind."

Scout looked like he was about to cry.

"Hey, we'll get you a new typewriter. An IBM."

"It's not the same. Man, it really pisses me off to think that gays would rip off their own kind."

"Wait a second. I thought you said there was no one here when you got home?"

"I did. They'd already left — the assholes. I hope somebody puts Armor All in their amyl ... fiberglass in their Lube..."

Nash cringed. "Jesus, Scout — I get the picture."

"I hope they get genital herpes!"

"Hey, back up a second. If they were already gone when you got here, how do you know they were *gay*?"

"Some detective *you'd* make. Didn't you notice that your *Colt* collection is missing?" It wasn't going to take Angela Lansbury to figure this one out. "So is the Erte in the hallway. *All* my Jane Oliver records!"

"Thank God," Nash murmured.

"All my Judy Garland albums. Aretha! Liza! Gladys! They cleaned me out!"

Nash darted to his bedroom. "Hey, they took all my gay porno!" He noticed the contents of his gym bag had been scattered about the floor. Something was missing. "They took my *jockstrap!*" He rushed back to the living room where Scout was standing, arms crossed against his chest.

"I rest my case."

He scratched his jaw. "I think you're right. Gays did rip us off."

"Not only that — didn't you even notice that all the living room furniture had been rearranged?"

Nash's eyes scanned the room. "Hey, it looks pretty good. Let's leave it this way."

Scout felt like Ricky in an episode of Lucy. All that was missing was Fred and Ethel.

# 17. Pink Power

At first, they were barely noticeable.

One was on the corner of Robertson and Santa Monica, eating at Lip Smackers.

Two were behind Video West, chatting in the alley.

Another one was window shopping at International Male.

A trio of muscular, intimidating males were stationed in the parking lot adjacent to Truffles.

Besides their sexual preferences, they had something else in common: they were all wearing Levis and powder pink Lacostes.

"Who are they?" Buddy asked, adjusting the Dodger's baseball cap Nash had given to him to conceal his bandaged cranium. They were returning from dinner at Truffles.

"Actually," Scout said, "it's all because of you."

"Me? What do you mean because of me?"

"Well, after the ... *accident*, some of the guys got together a coalition in your behalf."

"What?"

"The pink Lacostes are a sign of solidarity," Jesse added.

"Yeah," Scout continued, "I haven't seen the community this united since the Briggs Initiative. That's why everyone at Truffles was in pink. Didn't you notice how everyone was looking at you, Bud?"

Buddy scratched a tiny scar beneath his left eye. The scar resembled a scratch of premature crow's feet, offsetting his boyish looks with a dash of roguish charm.

"I did," he replied, "but I thought it was because of my bandages."

"No. You're their *cause célèbre*," Scout grinned.

"They even have a name," Jesse injected.

"A name?" Buddy wasn't enjoying this at all.

"You've heard of the Black Panthers?"

"And the Gray Panthers," Scout added. "Well, now there's the *Pink* Panthers!"

Buddy stopped in his tracks. "Scout, we have to talk."

Jesse sensed immediately that something was amiss.

Scout wasn't so perceptive. "Sure, Bud, but you haven't heard the latest. Two Pink Panthers attacked a white woman down on the boulevard the other night."

"They what?"

"Yeah. One held her down while the other one did her hair, makeup, and critiqued her ensemble."

Buddy looked pale.

"It's a joke, Bud! It's a joke!"

# 18. I've Got a Secret

Gloria Steinem would have wretched at Scout's antiquated kitchen philosophy: cooking was women's work — if Mrs. Paul or Sara Lee didn't make it, neither did he.

His knowledge of cuisine hadn't evolved one iota beyond Velveeta cheese sandwiches or the rudiments of what he considered the four basic food groups: frozen, bottled, canned or boxed.

Tonight, like an intrepid explorer of the vast unknown, he strayed from that theme and attempted the impossible — cooking from scratch.

Whatever it was Scout placed on the table reminded Buddy of a Hoosier cow pie from the cornfields of Indiana, freshly dropped and steaming. He had seen the hospital discard better looking meals than this one.

"*Viola!*" Scout stood back proudly from the table, removing a pair of trout-shaped pot holders.

The stumped expression of a game show contestant buzzed Buddy's face like a low flying plane. He tried to be as diplomatic as possible. "What is it?"

"Dinner!" Scout rubbed his hands together like the Big Bad Wolf about to dine on the Three Little Pigs.

"What exactly is it?"

"Give me a break," he moaned, expecting as much. "So it doesn't look like a Stouffer's picture — it's still edible."

That was not only debatable, but an understatement, not to mention a matter of opinion. Buddy peered suspiciously over the rim of his wine glass. "Is it supposed to be *that* color?"

"Yes, it's supposed to be *that* color," Scout mimicked wickedly, snapping a linen napkin across his lap. "Jesus, I spend all afternoon in a hot kitchen, and this is the thanks I get? If I had known this was going to be your attitude, we could have called *Chicken Delight!*"

Buddy guffawed. "All afternoon? Scout, you were only in there forty-five minutes."

"Everyone's a critic. What is this — the Betty Crocker Bake-Off or a quiet dinner between friends?"

"Scout, I was kidding."

"All right." He crossed-examined Buddy with the blink of an eye. "Can we eat now or are there any more comments?"

"Well..."

"Spit it out!"

That sounded like a good idea, but instead Buddy nodded toward the Corning Ware. "Just tell me what it is."

"Mystery casserole — now eat it!"

After dinner the powwow moved to the living room. In candle-light, Buddy sat with his back against the sofa, legs tucked under him yoga-style on the floor.

Scout's face became as wooden and distressed as the antique coffee table holding their coffee. "What?"

"That night I was attacked."

Scout nodded.

"I saw myself die, Scout."

"You what?"

"I died, Scout. I saw them bring me back to life, almost against my will."

"I don't understand, Buddy."

"I left my body. I saw everything. I saw Maizie, the crowds in the street, even the paramedics. I was dead, but I was watching it all. I *wanted* to die, but they told me to go back — that it wasn't time yet."

"What? *Who* told you to go back?"

"The voices ... in the light."

"Voices? You mean, the light from the ambulance? A voice from the crowd?"

Buddy shook his head. "Heavenly voices ... inside the light." His face glowed in remembrance. "The purest, most beautiful light I've ever seen, Scout. It was ... indescribable. As if all the answers to all the questions you'd ever want to ask were *inside* that light."

"Buddy," Scout whispered, leaning forward, "are you putting me on? This is a joke, right?"

"It happened, Scout. You're the first person I've told."

"Bud, I think we'd better keep this to ourselves for a while. This is too wild."

"Do you think I'm crazy, Scout?"

"Of course not. There's bound to be a reasonable explanation for this. I just can't think what it would be, that's all."

As Buddy cleared the dishes, Scout dragged from a cigarette as if it were a life support system, sifting through everything Buddy had told him. There was something about the phenomenon of people being pronounced clinically dead, then returning to tell about it, usually to the *National Enquirer*, but he couldn't remember where he'd read it.

Suddenly, in a flash of total recall, he remembered. He'd read it *in* the *National Enquirer*. He also remembered the juxtaposing article: *Kidnapped by Aliens*, about a Kalamazoo housewife who had supposedly taken a world tour with a friendly UFO.

Unnoticed, he stared at Buddy quizzically. Was this the famous fifteen minutes Andy Warhol once talked about? Was a headline in the *National Enquirer* going to be Buddy's claim to fame?

# 19. Rock the Box

"There's someone outside to see you, Dan. I told him to wait in the lobby."

Dan Carlton looked up from the menu of local disasters and international situations that would make up the afternoon's broadcast. As usual, the world was full of turmoil, with enough bad news to choke a masochist. One item in particular jumped from the page:

Jerry Falwell was closing down his *Gospel Hour's* toll-free hotline. It seemed the number was receiving an inordinate amount of calls from gay computer aces, who'd programmed their home systems to dial, every thirty seconds, the Evangelist's number. The result was a whopping two million dollar telephone bill, which put a smile on old Ma Bell's face, and a crimp in the cash flow of tax-free direct-dial religion. Jerry's hotline to God was apparently overloaded.

"Dan? He says he's a friend of yours."

"I'm busy, damnit. Tell him to make an appointment!"

"All right, but I think he said his name is Nash ... Aqua ... Aqualung or something like that."

The anchorman jumped to his feet. "Thanks. I'll take care of it."

He would have recognized that pumped-up physique anywhere.

"What the fuck are you doing here?"

Nash turned around as Dan grabbed a mound of bicep and pulled him into an empty hallway. "Hey, it's nice to see you, too."

"Damnit, Nash, I told you never to come here."

He jerked his arm away. "You did not!"

"Well, I meant to, then."

"Well, you *didn't!* And I didn't drive all the way to the valley in this heat for abuse. I get plenty of that from Scout."

"So what exactly are you doing here?"

"I wandered in on a studio tour — what do you think I'm doing here? I stopped by to take Johnny Carson to lunch, but he was busy, so I came looking for you."

Dan chewed his bottom lip. "I've already eaten."

"Great. Just point me towards a restroom and I'll be on my way. I've got to piss like a racehorse."

Dan looked both ways, like a child crossing a busy intersection. "Follow me."

Nash rolled his eyes, following him down a circuitous route away from the hubbub of the news room, up a flight of stairs, down a darkened corridor past deserted conference rooms, around a corner, and finally to an unmarked door.

"So this is where they've been hiding Cronkite!"

Dan wasn't amused. He shoved Nash into the room, locking the door behind them. Like a sentry in a maximum security prison, he watched sullenly from the door.

Peering sheepishly over his shoulder from a urinal, an Alfred E. Newman grin across his mouth, Nash beckoned the anxious anchorman over. "Hey, want to *shake* it?"

He obviously didn't. His carefully manicured moustache resembled a petrified caterpillar.

Nash shrugged. "Just thought I'd ask." Buttoning his fly, he joined Dan by the door. "How about a quickie?"

The anchorman recoiled. "Don't be absurd. I've got to get you out of here now without being seen."

Downstairs in the main lobby, a man in army fatigues and a semi-punk hairdo was scribbling in a cheap dimestore notebook. *Hollywood Tattletales* was stitched crudely across the back of his jacket in red lettering. His eyes instantly zoomed in on Dan Carlton and the handsome bodybuilder he was conversing with.

"Get this straight," Dan was saying. "I don't want you coming here again."

"Man, you're so paranoid," Nash retorted. "I hate to be the one to deflate your ego, but do you actually think anyone gives a flying fuck about who you're seen with?"

"*I* care — and I'm not paranoid. I'll talk to you later."

Nash watched him disappear, then headed towards the main doors. The man in army fatigues approached him as he was about to exit the building.

"Excuse me. Aren't you a bartender at Truffles?"

Nash paused.

"Wasn't that Dan Carlton, the anchorman, I saw you talking to just now?"

Nash glared at the cheap, frayed notebook, then fixed the man with a chilly stare. "Who are you supposed to be — Lois Lane?"

The smile on the man's face cracked. He quickly changed tactics. "Have you known Dan Carlton long?"

Nash's muscles tensed; his eyes narrowed. "Hey, I don't know you and you don't know me, so get the hell out of my way."

"You do work at Truffles, though."

Nash pushed open the doors. "Get lost, Bozo!"

# 20. Being There

Indiana, popularly known as the bouncing basketball capital of the free world, has also been called the armpit of the midwest. Visitors have regularly reported that the next best thing to being there is *leaving* there. Although any state with a city that goes by the name of *French Lick* can't be all bad.

Topographically speaking, Indiana has been given a bum rap. Its gently undulating hills, verdant countryside and cerulean skys are no less undulating, verdant or cerulean than its neighbors, Michigan and Ohio; it's autumnal colors no less picturesque than New England. Yet, if it was not the state itself, what exactly was it that prompted travelers to press both cheeks to cold glass and moon it from speeding cars?

Buddy Dove knew, and the onus pointed not toward Mother Nature but in an entirely different direction: Hoosiers. It was the general uptightness of the populace that made him queasy, that made his knees rattle and his heart throttle. He felt the same way about stumbling upon a barbecue thrown by the Klu Klux Klan. Nevertheless, it was (by no fault of his own) home.

"You can't be serious?" Scout put down the foil-like sun deflector he'd been holding under his chin. "Back to Indiana — the land that Time forgot! Why?"

"It's not *that* bad, Scout," Buddy laughed, positioning himself on the grass, a few feet from Scout's chaise longue.

"If it's not *that* bad," he mimicked, "then why'd you put roots down here in the first place?"

"Roots? I wouldn't exactly call an alarm clock and a suitcase of clothes ... *roots*."

"Have Nash and I done something? Don't you feel at home with us?"

"No. You and Nash have been great."

"Then what is it?" He sat up, causing a pool of sweat that had collected in his bellybutton to trickle to the elastic band of his Hawaiian print trunks.

"Everything." Buddy scratched his head; a patchy spot in

back hadn't quite caught up with the rest of his hair since leaving the hospital.

"Hey, it's not because of those roach-faced punks that beat up on you, is it?"

"Not exactly."

"Shoot, Bud, that could have happened anywhere. Even in Indiana. You were just in the wrong place at the wrong time."

"No, it's not just that."

"Then what?" Scout reached for his cigarettes.

Buddy hesitated. A blade of grass screamed silently as he yanked it from the lawn and put it between his lips.

"It's . . . I can't find . . . anyone."

"You mean, a boyfriend?"

He nodded sullenly.

"What about that guy Max? The dancer."

"He was already dating someone."

"Well, at least you finally got the nerve up to ask him out. That's a start. What happened to that guy you met at Studio One?"

"The Seville Sisters?"

"Huh?"

"The Seville Sisters — that's what I call him. He and his brother only date guys that drive Sevilles. I don't even have a car, much less a Cadillac."

"Well, you're always welcome to take mine. Maybe you should try the bars in the valley. I hear they're not as superficial out there."

"I'm sick of the bars, Scout. Besides, did *you* ever meet anyone in a bar that wanted a relationship?"

"Well, no, but. . ."

"Well, neither have I." Buddy spit out the blade of grass.

"I'm sure there must be guys out there that feel the same as you do, Bud. These things take time. Maybe you shouldn't be so . . . eager. Maybe when you *stop* looking, you'll find what you're looking for."

"I don't know. I think I should just go home."

"Give it a chance. At least wait until the gay parade before you start clicking your heels together and chanting 'There's no place like home.' Relax. You'll meet someone."

# 21. Shopping

Scout hadn't seen baskets that size since Easter.

They were standing by the Calvin Klein underwear display in the men's department of Neiman-Marcus. Buddy contented himself with cruising a life-sized poster of supermodel Tod Hintnaus that left little to the imagination.

A voice rang out from the crowd. "Scout!"

He turned to see who was calling, barely recognizing the woman approaching him. The fright wig of human hair had been shorn of its pop-art hues and was now dyed a toasty, autumn brown and cut stylishly close to her head.

"Justine? What happened? You look..."

"*Normal?*"

"I was going say different."

"Honey, I *am* different. I'm getting my act together and taking it on the road."

He half expected her to break into song.

"New York to be exact. L.A.'s turning my brains into Silly Putty. You know what Truman Capote said: 'It's a scientific fact that if you stay in California you lose one point of your I.Q. every year.' You can see what it's done to Ted."

"How is Ted?"

"We're getting a divorce. Didn't you know?"

"No. I'm sorry. That's too bad."

"Too bad for him," she smirked. "I caught him in bed with the gardener."

"Ted's *gay?*"

"The gardener's a woman, honey. I could have handled a man. I mean, there's no harm in experimentation, but another woman? That's where I draw the line. Anyway, I won't bore you with the details, but if you know of anyone that's interested in buying that elephant of a house, give them my number."

"Sure, Justine. I'll do that."

Heavy metal hit the floor with a clank. Nash moved in for a closer examination. "Is it Christmas already?"

"This is nothing," Buddy grinned. "You should've seen the stuff that got away."

Scout shrugged it off. "Some people do drugs. Some do booze. I prefer to shop."

Nash shook his head at all the packages. "Did you knock over a Brinks truck, or what?"

"Haven't you ever heard of deficit spending? The president does it all the time. Besides, it's the American way."

Nash still wasn't convinced. "What'd you use to pay for all this stuff?"

"Plastic," Scout winked. "Synthetic cash. Why? Are you writing a book, too?"

"Testy little cocksucker, ain't he?" Nash joked, joining Buddy on the sofa. "What are you going to use to pay for all this when the bills start rolling in?"

"I've got some stories coming out, all right?"

"Not more Harlequin romances — why do you write that drivel?"

"Listen, I'd write douche commercials if it'd pay the rent. Besides, Mickey Spillane said, 'If they pay you for it, nothing is schlock.'"

"He should know."

"Anyway, you can't put a price tag on love."

"They do in Boys' Town," Buddy injected.

"That's *sex,*" Scout reprimanded.

Is all this stuff for Jesse?" Nash asked, examining the price tag on a wafer-thin gold watch. "He's a nice guy, but let's face it, you haven't known him very long."

"Ha! *You* should talk!" Scout countered. "How long have you known that closet queen newscaster?"

"He's *not* a closet queen!" Nash replied staunchly.

"Give me a break, Nash. Anyone that comes and goes by the back door, parks his car two blocks from the house and *refuses* to be seen with you in natural light is either a closet queen or a vampire."

Buddy's head swiveled between his friends like a spectator's at Wimbledon.

"I have to admit," Scout continued, "it's nice to see you finally relinquish your title as champion sport-fucker. For a while there I thought we'd have to install a revolving door on your bedroom. At least he's an improvement over your last semi-serious affair."

Nash feigned amnesia. Unfortunately, his housemate had the memory retrieval of an elephant — he never forgot.

"You remember," Scout prompted, "*Paulo* — the Colt model. The one with an ego too big for his gym shorts."

Nash dissolved into the sofa.

Buddy was incredulous. "*You* dated a Colt model?"

"He sure did," Scout grinned. Dishing Nash's sex life was almost as much fun as shopping. "Paulo a.k.a. Ralph, from Waxahachie Falls, Mississippi. Can you believe it?"

Buddy was all ears.

"You know that gorilla, Koko — the one they're teaching to communicate with flash cards? Well, old Paulo had a lot in common with Koko — he was just as hairy and almost as smart!"

"The word I'm thinking of at this moment," Nash joked, "rhymes with witch."

"Oh, come on, Nash. Ralph ... Excuse me, *Paulo*, was as common as restroom graffiti and about as original, too. And, his IQ. Well, his IQ is legendary."

Nash guffawed. He knew what was coming.

Buddy was on Tokyo time. "What about his IQ?"

Scout's eyebrows shot to his hairline. "It matched his pecker — they were both a perfect twelve!"

"Hey," Nash laughed, "when you have a body like Paulo's, it doesn't matter what comes out of your mouth."

"I doubt if there was much thought about what went into it either."

"That's not fair, Scout. So Paulo never read Aeschylus or Euripides — that doesn't make him stupid."

"True, but when he misses two out of three on *Family Feud*, that has to tell you something. Poor Paulo couldn't sell dollar bills for ninety cents on Wall Street!"

"Man, you're such a snob. Steve Schulte was a Colt model, and he went to *Yale*! Plus, he's a respected member of the gay community, too."

"Steve Schulte is an anomalous exception. Paulo, unfortunately, is the norm."

Nash crossed his arms and sat back. "You're jealous!"

"Hardly. Even if Dan Carlton is a closet queen, he at least keeps you off the streets."

"Screw you!" Nash snapped in mock reproach.

"And ruin my reputation?"

"What reputation?"

"As one of the few you haven't gotten between the sheets!"

Buddy's face took on the color of a pointsettia at Christmas. "Oops!"

Nash shifted uncomfortably on the sofa. "Well, miracles do happen. It just took me awhile to find the right man. No offense, Bud."

"Well, it ain't for lack of trying. And I haven't seen a miracle like *that* since Jennifer Jones picked up a faggot and saw the Madonna in *The Song of Bernadette!*"

Nash got up and resumed his workout. "You can be a real *cunt* sometimes. I think it's all those Twinkies and junk food — you're having withdrawals. Bud, you'd better call City Hall and alert the mayor."

"Hey, I just call them as I see them."

"Then, you'd better get a new prescription for your glasses."


# 22. Two Men in a Tub

Nina Simone, Gladys Knight and Anita Baker sang love songs in the background, via a Sony tape deck, with a worldiness unheard of in the saccharine strains of a Manilow or Newton-John. It was soulful, black and beautiful.

Roederer's Cristal sparkled in fluted glasses like rare liquid diamonds, refracting rays of flickering light from myriad candles of cinnamon, vanilla and spice, premeating the bathroom with a sweet, patchouli scent.

Jackson's Mr. Bubble produced the luxurious bathtub spume in which the two men were semi-submerged.

Jesse lowered the crystal gingerly from his lips. A queer, bemused smile was crinkling Scout's lips. His lover seemed lost in a dream.

"What are you thinking?"

Scout's eyes fluttered open. Grandly, he lifted his glass to his lips and sipped. "This must be what it feels like to be Zsa Zsa Gabor. Champagne and bubbles and the man that you love."

Jesse shook his head. "You're nuts."

Jesse rotated a loofah around the smooth plane of his lover's back. "Don't stop. Finish your story."

"What was I saying?"

"Steve Reeves."

"Oh, yeah. Good old Steve," Scout sighed. "Nash and I had the biggest crush on him when we were kids. He was such a hunk — the Schwarzenegger of the fifties. We'd spend an entire Saturday afternoon at the Rivoli, watching him flex in all of those Hercules movies. Man, could he *act!* What about you?"

"I had a crush on Sandra Dee."

"That's a coincidence — there was a time I thought I *was* Sandra Dee!"

"Come on."

"I'm not kidding. While Connie and I worried about *Where the Boys Are,* you were busy drooling over pintsized poontang."

"Lucky for you it was just a stage I was going through. Tell me some more."

"What's to tell? I suffered through your average, gay adolescence. I tell you, puberty was one perpetual erection."

"Did you date any girls?"

"Girls!!" Scout turned to him in mock-horror. "Wash your mouth out with soap!"

"Oh, Scout. You must have dated one girl during high school."

"Excuse me? Sushi is an acquired taste, not unlike caviar."

"I don't believe you."

"Actually, I did date *one* girl, although I would have preferred the captain of the football team, but I think Nash was dating him."

"I knew it. Tell me all the gory details."

"There's not much to tell. I dated her until I discovered she was only after one thing."

"Which was?"

"To get into my britches."

"Be serious."

"I *am* serious! That girl not only grew up to burn her bra, but to head the ERA. I'm sure of it. She sure as hell didn't need liberating. You, of all people, should know how *they* are. Man, once they get a whiff of it, they're all over you like an octopus — arms everywhere but where they should be. And, once they finally do get into your pants, it's good-bye respect. They start trashing your reputation in the locker room after volley ball practice. Word gets out and then they figure you're an easy mark. McDonald's and a movie and they think they own you. Pretty soon, it gets around school that you have peanut butter legs, and you're dead meat."

Jesse chuckled. "Peanut butter legs — what's that?"

"You know — they *spread* easily."

"Will you be serious."

"I am being serious. You give them a little nookie in a weak moment, and the next thing you know you're the town scandal. Branded a hussy!"

After several moments of quiet contemplation, Jesse easily concluded that Mona Lisa's cheeks had nothing on Scout's. Ultimately, as if to corroborate his suspicions, he planted a tender but manly kiss on his lover's derriere.

Scout purred like a kitten on cashmere. Turning onto his back, he reached up and pressed his hand, thumb, index finger and pinkie up, middle two fingers down, against the tanned flesh of Jesse's pecs.

It was sign language from *Torch Song Trilogy*. Jesse recognized it immediately. They had seen it together with Harvey Fierstein reprising his Tony-winning role. "I love you, too," Jesse murmured, snuggling up beside him. "Now, tell me what's on your mind."

"Jesus, you and Nash can read me like a book."

"Well, what is it?"

"Oh ... *Everything!* Buddy's talking about moving back to Indiana."

"Why?"

"Because he can't seem to find a boyfriend."

"Oh. Those things take time."

"That's what I told him. And Dan is talking about taking Nash to Hawaii. I think Nash may even move in with him."

"What else?"

"I don't know. But I do know I'd like to be able to take *you* to Hawaii."

"I'm happy right where I am."

"Me, too, but I want more for us."

"Maizie says that if you've got your health, you ain't got no reason to be singin' the blues. Some people don't even have that."

"I know."

Jesse searched his lover's face for the fatal trace of discontentment — the gypsy feet syndrome commonly prevalent among gay relationships. "Are you trying to tell me the honeymoon is over?"

"God, no!" Scout bolted upright. "Are you kidding? I'm in this for the duration. I just want to give you the world on a silver platter, but all I can afford right now is Fiestaware."

Jesse hugged him. "You're nuts."

"Yeah, did I tell you Ted and Justine's house is up for sale, too?"

"No. But so what?"

"This is the *nuts* part. I want to buy it so we can all live together."

"How much are they asking for it?"

"$195,000."

"You're right — you are nuts."

# 23. The Dating Game

Scout was at Jesse's. Nash was behind the bar at Truffles, and Buddy had the entire house to himself.

Fresh from the shower, a towel wrapped around his waist, he paced the living room leaving a sweet scent of Eau Sauvage trailing behing him. Deliberating on what had to be done, *Aretha's Gold* on the stereo helped to put him in the *doing* mood.

He walked the few feet to the dining room table and sat down. He reached for the telephone, touched it, then as if the touch of cold plastic repelled him, nervously wiped his hand across his terryclothed thighs.

Taking a deep, exaggerated breath, he unfolded a worn piece of paper with a name and telephone number on it. Gingerly, he dialed the number written beneath the name Raphael.

On the third ring, Buddy lowered his voice to a manly but unnatural baritone. "Raphael? This is Buddy." A slight pause followed.

As brief as the pause was, it nevertheless filled Buddy's solar plexus with a queasiness the size of a head of Iceberg lettuce. He could almost detect the clicking of gears as the callee's mind raced to place an unfamiliar voice and name with a face. He shifted uncomfortably in the chair, already sweating. He wasn't sure if the voice in the background was that of another man or just a TV.

Finally, the voice of Raphael spoke. "Ummm, can you refresh my memory?"

Buddy feigned an unconvincing laugh, a laugh that often accompanies embarrassment but does precious little to conceal it, much like a bumblebee trying to conceal an elephant. It had the same effect.

"Oh," he started, feeling like Hulk Hogan at a Mensa meeting, "well, we met the other night at Rage. I was dancing with a black girl who thought she was Diana Ross, when you cut in."

"Oh, yeah, the drag queen."

"I beg your pardon."

"You were dancing with that drag queen from Four Star."

"I was?" Buddy had no idea that the woman he'd danced with was a man.

"So," Raphael said, "how are you, Bobby?"

Buddy swallowed. "It's *Buddy!*"

"So how are you?"

"I'm fine. I was just wondering if you'd like to take in a movie tonight ... Remember ... you told me to call you sometime."

"Gee..."

"Buddy!"

"Right — Buddy. Gee, I'm sort of tied up tonight."

Buddy thought he probably *was* tied up tonight. He looked like the bondage type. Raphael was obviously out of his league.

He would have had better luck calling the drag queen.

"Oh, I understand. Maybe another time."

"Sounds good. Why don't you call me next week and we'll get together then."

Buddy didn't think so, but lied through his teeth anyway. "I'll do that, Raphael. Bye."

Ma Bell had let him down — he'd reached out to touch someone, but the someone had no desire to touch back.

He debated the idea of going to the movies alone, but the debate ended two seconds later. He wasn't going to the movies alone. Movies for one was about as enticing as sex with a chain saw.

Instead, he walked to the bedroom and a stack of magazines, pulling out the current issue of *Torso*. He began leafing through the magazine until he came to a photograph of a healthy-looking blond.

Tonight, his date was on page seventy-two.

# 24. Lover's Quarrel

Nash hadn't experienced such boredom since *Heaven's Gate*. Waiting around for Dan Carlton was becoming a real ball and chain. Since meeting the anchorman, he had turned down innumerable dates: a trip to Acapulco, the Russian River, New York and the sedulous advances of a porno producer that had promised the stalwart bartender: "I'll make you a star, babe!"

And, for what? A relationship that existed on the slim scenario of carnal interludes in a bedroom? Sex that was so incidental that it fit into an integral whole of nothing? If less was more, then he had the whole enchilada.

The play of the field was beckoning him to return to a stellar cast of Boys' Town finest: MEN — One size fits all!

Scout, who could never drop his drawers and throw his legs to the wind, who couldn't fathom sex without love (an antiquated notion if Nash ever heard one), had held out for his ideals and found them in Jesse.

He, on the other hand, had strayed from what seemed his charted course. Never one for the romance of human commitment, he'd fallen into a somewhat compromising situation with L.A.'s closet newsman.

Something had to give and soon. He was getting cabin fever of the loins.

There was a light on in the house when the green Mercedes pulled into the driveway. A cloak of darkness canceled any misgivings Dan Carlton might have had of being seen in the gay ghetto.

Nash met him at the door with a scowl. "You were supposed to be here at nine o'clock!" He glared at the anchorman, then at his watch. "It's now eleven minutes past midnight. I don't need this aggravation in my life!"

"I know — I should have called you."

"Damn right you should have called me!" The veins in his neck strained in bas-relief. Dan started towards him, but a sturdy hand kept him at bay.

Nash grabbed a stone-washed denim jacket from the sofa and threw it over his shoulder.

"Where are you going?"

"Out! To the goddamn bars!"

Dan momentarily flushed with anger. His moustache twitched as he tried to control himself. "Listen . . . I'm sorry."

Nash displayed about as much movement as the Rock of Gibraltar.

"If you'll calm down and get me a drink, I'll explain. It's been a hectic day — don't make it any worse."

Nash folded his arms across his chest.

"I could really use that drink."

Stoically, Nash went to the kitchen and got a beer from the refrigerator. "Here," he barked, throwing the can in Dan's direction. "Drink it on your way out of here!"

"Hey!" Dan caught it with one hand. "Damnit, let me explain!"

"Tell it to my ass," Nash sneered. "I'm going out!"

The look on the anchorman's face could have broken glass. He lurched for Nash's arm as he passed, catching a fistful of bicep, and flung him to the sofa.

Fists clenched, Nash jumped up, but Dan shoved him down fast.

"This macho crap doesn't work with me, mister!"

"Up yours!" Nash's biceps flexed, loosening Dan's grip. He was ready to duke it out, whatever the hazards.

Fuming, the anchorman pulled back. His libido was making an emergency call south of the border, and as usual, his libido was calling the shots. His tone softened. "Let's discuss this like rational human beings."

There are more than fifty alphabets in the world.

Among the myriad forms of expression, the most common is the systematic communication by vocal symbols; a universal characteristic among Homo sapiens, not limited to Homo sapien homosexuals. This was Nash and Dan's immediate choice, although Nash did most of the talking.

Dan listened, suppressing an ego that was not to be taken lightly beneath a practiced demeanor to temperate cool.

Next, there is body language — tactile dialect that is usually learned at puberty and continued and refined through adult life. Both men were adept at this physical lexicon, although Nash had clearly gone on for his doctorate, while Dan had remained content with a mere B.A. It was this latter form of communication that broke the cold front separating them.

Nash felt like he'd been hit by a steamroller. His heart was still pounding beneath the sculptured mass of hirsute pectorals when he leaned across Dan's body for a cigarette.

"I think it's time we took that trip to Hawaii. We need some quality time to ourselves."

Nash was feeling too good to argue.

"I'll make the reservations. When do you want to leave?"

"Anytime after Sunday. I can't go before the gay parade."

Dan was silent.

Nash knew what he was thinking. "If you'll go to the gay parade, I'll fly to Hawaii with you."

"We've discussed *that* already."

"Listen, I'm getting tired of playing by *your* rules. I think it's about time you began playing by mine."

Dan got up and started dressing. "I'll think about it."

Nash glared at him. "You do that." Dan Carlton was like a tree that would rather break than give. The survival of their relationship was in jeopardy.

Rita Mae Brown had compared relationships to "sprints" and "marathons." Theirs had gone beyond the sprint, but Nash seriously doubted if there was enough life left in it to go the distance. Dan Carlton just refused to bend, in more ways than one.

# 25. And So It Goes

They were lunching alfresco at The Greenery.

The sidewalk, inches from their table, resembled a runway of truant gymthusiasts and Bryman renegades. The beautiful and the butch were out in force.

"It's like Bette Davis and Warner Brothers in the thirties."

Buddy wasn't exactly sure what point Scout was trying to make. "Huh?"

He may not have had Bette Davis's eyes, but their lungs could've been twins. He lit another cigarette and inspected the almost empty package. "Well, you've got a lot on the ball, a lot to offer, but all you're getting is lousy B-movie scripts." He nibbled on a greasy tuna melt; adjusted his glasses. "We're a dying breed, Buddy. We belong in the Smithsonian, next to Archie Bunker's chair. Face it, we're in love with love."

"That's easy for you to say. You've got Jesse."

"And I'm grateful as hell *to* have him, but after Noah died, I didn't see anyone for two years. Believe me, I know how you feel."

Buddy sipped his iced tea. "I wish I knew how *you* feel."

"You will. You've got to have more patience than patience itself. The right man *will* come along. He's out there waiting for you somewhere."

"Well, I wish somebody would tell him where I live!"

"Stop trying so hard. Whatever happened to just dating someone and getting to know them before having sex? Who said you have to go to bed with somebody first and get to know them later? Gays have it all backwards. Ass-backwards, to be precise."

"But it's *expected*. That's the way it is."

"Bullshit, Buddy. You're suffering from Toxic Cock Syndrome."

"*Scout!*"

"Excuse me, but it's true. Let's face it, you haven't exactly been Chastity Chaste the last few weeks. Just because you're ready to throw in the towel and hightail it back to the electric cornfield — which I happen to think is a big mistake on your part — what did Indiana ever do for you? Are the pickin's any better back there?"

"No."

"I rest my case."

"But..."

"But nothing. Relax and let nature take its course."

# 26. Lost and Found

It was, by all accounts, a red letter day for celebrity watching.

The sky was an unusually clear palette of cerulean *infinitum*, without the faintest fuzz of smog.

Buddy left the gym in high spirits. The sun felt good across his face and neck as he headed towards Boys' Town.

The storefronts blurred as he passed. Unity Savings & Loan, Mrs. Field's Cookies, Animal Farm, Video Ga Ga...

He spotted her coming out of Shatsky & Shapiro, a funky five-and-dime that reminded him of Walgreen's back in Indiana. It was Lily Tomlim, walking directly in front of him.

She was smiling as she glanced over her shoulder.

"Hi," he said, self-consciously.

"Hello. Hello. How are you?" she smiled.

Startled, Buddy laughed. "Great. How are you?"

"Just terrific," she grinned, an indescribable brio igniting her face. "Well," she said, heading for the crosswalk, "Have a nice day."

He shook his head in amazement, coursing down the boulevard, with an added skip to his gait. Things like this sure didn't happen in Indiana.

Further on down the street, Maxfield Bleu was having a sale. He decided to look inside.

Upon entering the black matte door his eyes locked on a dazzlingly handsome dark-haired man. He tried not to stare, but his eyes refused to disconnect from the strikingly handsome profile. Briefly the man looked up, smiled, then resumed rummaging through a bulky heap of expensively marked sweaters.

A clerk with go-go pink lips, wearing a knotted t-shirt dress and paisley hose, darted to his side and quickly hustled him off to a far corner of the store.

"That's Boy George," she whispered. "You know — Culture Club."

Buddy glanced discreetly across the room. Sure enough, it *was* Boy George, although he was much taller than Buddy had expected.

"That's Jon Moss — the drummer," she said sotto voce, pointing a diamond-embedded pink nail towards the dark-haired vision that had initially caught Buddy's eye. "Isn't he dreamy?"

"I'll say," Buddy murmured, corroborating her opinion.

This made her giggle. "It takes one to know one, huh?" She gave Buddy a blatant once over. "I mean, you're kind of dreamy yourself."

Buddy laughed out loud. His workouts at the gym were paying off. "Thanks."

A few blocks past the Pacific Design Center, he came upon a store he'd never seen before. It looked interesting, so he entered, following an instinct that usually led him to bargains and sales and purchases he didn't really need or want, but ended up buying because the markdown price was too seductive to pass by.

Chimes echoed in the air as the door to the Bodhi Tree closed behind him. The smooth scent of Indian sandalwood permeated the store, creating a kind of olfactory nirvana for the proboscis. Random rays of sunlight hit hanging crystals and slashed rainbows indiscriminately against the walls.

Since he was already inside, he decided to look around. He had never seen a store like this one back home.

The plethora of books ranged from food-combining to astral travel; from pyramid power to life before birth. Buddy had never seen anything like it. He returned a book to the shelf just in time to glance up and see a gamine redhead with a sprightly dancer's step hurry through the door.

"That's Shirley MacLaine," a voice whispered behind him.

Buddy smiled. The man addressing him looked like a blond Odom angel.

"You have a beautiful aura," the man said, through a sunny, Apollonian smile. Pale ash-blond hair swept lightly over his forehead to blue eyes and a Gallic nose.

A lump caught in Buddy's throat as his eyes brushed against the bare skin of golden pectorals beneath the opened folds of the man's shirt. "I'm sorry. What'd you say?"

"You have a nice aura."

If this was a come on, it was a new one to Buddy, but it sure as hell beat "Hey, kid, wanna sit on my face?"

"I do?" he asked, unsure of what an aura was, and surprised that anyone from Indiana would even have one. He decided to fake it. "What's it look like?"

"Do you have a minute?"

I've got a lifetime, he thought. "Sure."

"Let's go get some coffee."

Mesmerized, Buddy nodded.

"By the way, I'm Caleb Alexander."

# 27. Christopher Street West

They were dancing in the streets.

Gays were calling out around the world; West Hollywood was only one of many ports of call.

The boulevard was a hotbed of activity. Potential *Playgirl* centerfolds roamed the parade route with jocular camaraderie. Crowds had been queuing along the parade route since early morning in anticipation of the big day.

Parents displayed celebratory solidarity with their lesbian and gay offspring, some of whom were parents themselves, causing a nonpartisan observer of the festivities to murmur aloud: "Now I know how Dorothy felt in Munchkinland!"

There were butch dykes; lipstick dykes; Dykes on Bikes dykes. A bouillabaisse of gay men and women with a common cause: no one wanted it to rain on *their* parade.

Except for the doomsayers stationed across the street from the International House of Pancakes (the only flat note in the proceedings), the Christopher Street West Gay Parade had all the joviality of a Mardi Gras.

A man in Joan Crawford drag whizzed past the *Repent Now!* placards on roller-skates, towing a bearded man-child in a blonde marcelled wig with a wire hanger projecting from his curls like antenna. The flock of anti-gay demonstrators made Joan's padded shoulders quake. She yanked her daughter's training leash, signaling her to vamoose, but her hairy-legged sibling was intrepid in the face of such blatant anti-ness. She hiked her petticoats up and flashed the jeering penitents with a set of family jewels that left their mouths gaping.

"Arrest the pervert!" someone shrieked from the throng of placards.

"We're all God's children," shot a reply. "Fuck off!"

Roars of approval pealed from the bleachers along the boulevard as Joan and her daughter burned rubber towards Boys' Town.

A Boy George impersonator with an "I'll Tumble 4 Ya" look in his mascaraed eyes passed Jesse and Scout and Maizie on the street, zapping them merrily with confetti. Jackson, high atop his father's shoulders, squealed with boyish delight.

Maizie elbowed Scout's ribs. "This shindig reminds me of my son's wedding. That was a circus, too!"

Grinning, Scout looped his arm through hers as they walked. "I didn't know you had a son."

"I told you, there's a lot you don't know about me."

Jesse pointed to a huge, flamingo-pink monolith on wheels. "Look, there's Nash and Buddy."

A platoon of classically sculptured Pink Panthers flanked the float like centurions of Rome, which was a leviathan papier-mâché fist wielding a pink baseball bat of monstrously phallic proportions. The float's banner announced in bold letters: SWISH SOFTLY BUT CARRY A BIG STICK!

Maizie snapped a picture with her Kodak.

Nash, stationed aboard the float as one of Buddy's sentinals, diligently aligned a pink bikini with his tan line.

Buddy spotted them and waved, embarrassed that they had to see him enthroned in pink papier-mâché. He felt like the last Homecoming Queen. He smiled nervously as Maizie snapped his picture.

"Something for the folks back home," she smiled, snapping away.

"Nash! They're here," Buddy said through smiling lips, prodding his muscular guard with a glittered magic wand.

Nash quickly surveyed the crowd, but his eyes went beyond his friends, searching for a face that wasn't there.

The celebration continued in the parking lot behind the Pacific Design Center, a blue whale of a landmark known to cinema aficionados as *the* place where Margaux Hemingway blew away Chris Sarandon's pecker in her motion picture debut, *Lipstick*, causing critics to astutely note that considering Margaux's acting ability, the rifle was pointing in the wrong direction.

Everyone waited inside the gate for Nash and Buddy to de-float and change into street clothes.

When they arrived, an irritable despondency projected from Nash's physiognomy as clearly as the miniature alligator perched on the mound of his left pectoral.

Scout elbowed Buddy. "Who put a bug up his ass?"

"Dan Carlton was a no show."

"Shoot, I could have told him *that*. That man's going to suffocate if he doesn't come out of that closet he's in."

"He didn't exactly *say* he would be here. Anyway, you have to put yourself in his shoes."

"Hey, don't defend the prick! Nash is your friend, too!"

"I know," Buddy replied, casually making eye contact with a portly, gray-haired friar who was cruising Nash severely. Almost reverently.

"The trouble with this town," Scout continued, "is that everyone in the industry — movies, TV and recording business alike

— knows who's gay, but it's all right as long as they remain in the closet. I wish someone had the balls to come out publicly. All this hypocrisy really burns my ass!"

"Oh, climb off your soapbox for a while," Maizie said blithely, "and have a good time."

"Nash can look out for himself," Buddy offered.

The friar was slowly inching his way towards them.

"Hey, I've known him since kindergarten — you think I don't know that?" Scout countered.

Suddenly, the bogus clergyman was upon them. His eyes were fixed on Nash, like he was considering a sacrifice.

"Having a good time, brother?"

Nash fried him with a look that could have melted butter. "Yeah. I'm delirious — can't you tell?"

"And, what's your name, son?"

"That's Nash," Buddy offered, an impish gleam in his eyes.

The friar quickly grabbed Nash's hand, pressed his robed, round body up against the sculptured musculature and pulled him to his lips.

Scout's eyes looked like dinner plates. "Did you see that?" he said, elbowing Maizie.

"I'm not blind," she snapped.

Shocked, Nash forced the balding wrinkled face from his mouth. The friar had slipped him the *tongue*.

The disguise didn't fool Buddy for long. "It's Dan!" he laughed.

"*What?*" Nash was stunned.

The bold priest was Dan Carlton, incognito.

The anchorman pulled two first class tickets to Hawaii from his robes and winked at Nash. "Want to get *leied?*"

# 28. Love at Second Sight

He knew exactly how Mildred Pierce felt.

Truffles' lunchtime rush gradually slowed to a crawl. And not too soon. His feet felt like two baked potatoes. But it had been a good afternoon, with nearly seventy-five dollars in tips. After squaring with his busboy, slipping him an extra five, Buddy headed toward the front door but was called by another waiter named Andy.

"Hey, Buddy, how about covering dinner for me tonight?"

"I can't, Andy. Why don't you ask Pete?"

"I did. He told me to ask you."

"I can't. *Really.* I've got a date."

"I'll make it worth your while."

Buddy didn't see the tiny glass vial Andy pulled from his shirt pocket. He was already out the door.

There was something indefinable and electric about Caleb Alexander, something Buddy couldn't put his finger on. Their rapport had been instantaneous and magnetic, which was nothing new in Boys' Town. It happened all the time, like clockwork, but this was something different. It was their second date, and neither of them had dropped their drawers.

Buddy learned that Caleb was twenty-nine years old, had given up a Harvard-trained career in international law for a prestigious New York firm, and had traveled extensively throughout the Orient, Asia and Europe before putting down roots in California. Had it not been for Caleb's genuine indifference to his accomplishments, Buddy might have felt like an underachiever. As it was, he couldn't take his eyes from his companion's disarming smile.

Buddy waited in the patio, a small area off Caleb's living room, insulated by a plethora of plants and blooming flowers. A miniature stone Buddha meditated in the far corner, serenely tranquil in the idyllic surroundings.

Caleb soon joined him, pulling on a shirt. "Did you go to the gay parade?"

"Yeah. I went with my roommates." He was almost afraid to ask. "Did you go?"

"No. I couldn't go this year."

Buddy was relieved. "It was an experience. They sure don't have anything like it in Indiana."

Caleb laughed. "I bet. It's a whole different world out here. It sure as hell beats Boston. I think my parents get typhus shots before each visit. Luckily, for you, you just missed them. They won't be out again until next year."

Buddy smiled. He was thinking of his own family. It would definitely be a culture shock for old Irene and Howard to find him living in a house full of males in a community full of homosexuals.

"So," Caleb said, "I thought we'd drive out by the ocean and have dinner, then afterwards we can walk along the beach in the moonlight. How's that sound?"

Romantic, Buddy thought. "It sounds great."

Caleb leaned over and kissed him gently on the lips. Buddy's heart melted. His pulse raced. He felt like he was sitting on the electric chair and the warden had turned on the juice. He felt the earth move under his feet. He felt the family jewels turn into a fountain pen. He prayed that it wouldn't leak!

# 29. Up, Up and Away

Minutes before takeoff, after diligently perusing the candy and chewing gum selection in the airport gift shop, Jackson joined his father at the magazine rack where he was selecting reading material for his friend's flight to Hawaii.

"Hey, Pop!"

Jesse glanced down at the familiar greeting. Jackson's fists were crammed with an assortment of candy and gum.

"Hey, didn't I tell you *no* candy? One pack of gum and it'd better be sugarless," he said authoritatively.

Jackson rolled his eyes, mumbling a preschool obscenity as he returned to the candy counter. "Ya old dickhead!"

Dan Carlton, waiting nervously behind a pair of black wraparound Yoko Ono sunglasses, waited across the room, shielding his locally famous face behind a copy of *The Wall Street Journal*.

Not far from him, Scout cornered Nash with last-minute instructions. "Be sure and call when you arrive — let it ring twice so we'll know you got there all in one piece."

"Savvy."

"And, don't overdo it the first day in the sun. And take plenty of vitamin B."

"Savvy."

"Got the tickets?"

"Dan has them."

"Oh, I almost forgot." He stuffed a folded twenty dollar bill in Nash's shirt pocket. "Jackson wants a coconut head."

Nash started to retrieve the money. "I think I can afford that."

Scout pushed his hand back down. "Then, buy whatshisname a couple of cocktails. He looks like he could use them!"

In a world where precious few are equal and little is free (and what appears to be free usually has strings attached), the sun, 865,400 miles in diameter, balanced high and free in the clear skies above the Maui/Lanai/Molokai triangle, like a bald fried egg (sunny side up).

The celestial furnace, free from the mundane prejudices of the earthly kind, was unequivocably egalitarian: it burned, baked, fried and peeled without the slightest regard to race, creed or sexual preference — no strings attached. Its torridness shimmered like the insides of a red-hot chili pepper.

The magnificent bombardment of its penetrating ultraviolets stretched magnanimously over the secluded bay of archipelagos to tourists and natives alike, throughout the exotic Rousseau-like foliage of the Aloha State to the South Pacific and all points beyond.

Dan Carlton felt like a new man as he stood on the bedroom terrace overlooking the secluded bay, its beautiful scenery seemingly untouched by man's clawing hands. His beachfront property looked like a painting by Gauguin.

The lushness of the tropical environment had a liberating effect on him. The shackles of a career and dubious lifestyle had been temporarily severed. He felt like the last mango in paradise.

Behind him was a rustle of bed sheets. Nash looked up from a post-coitus hairdo, stretching his muscular arms.

Dan turned and smiled.

"I like that outfit," Nash grinned. "You should wear it more often."

Dan was standing before God and nature in nothing more than his birthday suit.

"*Au naturel* becomes you."

Dan looked out towards the bay. "Want to go for a swim?"

"Yeah, if you wear that bathing suit I bought for you."

"That thing's a visual obscenity."

"*Yeah!*" Nash leered at him like the Marquis de Sade. "I had to go to Frederick's of Hollywood for that little gem."

Dan held up the cheetah-print visual obscenity. "I thought I'd go as I am."

"Come on, wear it. Sometimes a little bit of clothing is sexier than wearing nothing at all."

"*Little* is right. That thing's disgusting."

"Put it on." He was practically drooling. "Then you can pretend you're Deborah Kerr and I'm Burt Lancaster."

"*You* can be Deborah Kerr — I'll be Burt."

"Have it your own way." Nash's brows did a little fertility dance above his eyes. Obviously, once was not enough. "Or maybe we could *both* be Burt."

"Don't tell me the natives are restless again?"

"Squeeze the horn of plenty into the suit of skimpy and I'll show you." He jumped out of bed and disappeared down the stairs.

Dan flinched, inspecting the nylon tricot swatch.

"Put it on!" a voice yelled from outside.

Dan moved to the terrace. Nash was on the beach, hands cupped around his mouth Tarzan-style. "Surf's up," he yelled. "Last one in the bay is a condom sniffer!" Then, like a spirited white-assed deer, he turned and sprinted into the azure waters.

Resignedly, Dan slipped the suit up his thighs, complaining aloud. "Jiminy Cricket couldn't fit into this thing!"

A chameleon darted across the hardwood floors.

Mozart wafted from the beach house on the arm of a warm afternoon breeze with graceful syncopation.

Nash plopped on the beach towel next to his Hawaiian companion. "You're getting burned. Want me to put some lotion on you?"

Dan hummed.

"Hey," Nash laughed, smoothing Bain de Soleil down the manly taper of Dan's back to his cheetah trunks. "You're getting hot cross buns!"

Dan sighed dramatically into the beach towel. Nash was pulling his trunks down around his ankles.

"If they come off," a sinister voice threatened, "you'll have to pay the consequences."

"Oh, yeah?"

"Yeah!" Dan lunged for him, pulling him to the towel with a real *From Here To Eternity* kiss. The surf lapped at their feet. The cheetah was ready to pounce.

High in the surrounding hills of yellow ginger blossoms, limpy koa trees and rainbow variegation of exotic flowers and verdant fern fronds, a mongoose looked on unsuspectingly. With a twinkle it scurried up the hill.

The natives were restless, but if God was watching, He didn't seem to mind.

# 30. Prognosis Negative

Dr. Dick Webster suffered from unnatural natural beauty. *Playgirl* had once displayed his credentials in a prominent centerfold that had set the gay community on its collective ear, causing hearts and libidos to palpitate with Concorde flights of fantasy. A sexy Scavullo-type photograph appeared religiously in *The Advocate*, extolling, if not his rumored bedside manner, his dedication to the Hippocratic Oath.

Dick Webster was a fledgling in the branch of medical science known as psychoneuroimmunology, and Caleb liked him because the doctor thought that medicine should build a patient's health through proper diet and hygiene, resorting to more drastic treatment only when absolutely necessary. The doctor was a firm believer in the hypothesis that the body's immune system could be affected by a patient's inner state of mind.

"As far as I can tell, the enlargement of the lymph nodes haven't regressed. I'd like to get you back into the hospital and run some more tests to be sure."

Caleb, who had been in and out of the hospital for the past year, wasn't so sure. He wasn't going back unless it was absolutely necessary. "I feel fine."

The doctor stroked his square matinee-idol jaw. "There will be times when you *do* feel fine, Caleb. You know that. But..."

"But, I'm going to die. I'm *dying* as we speak. I know, I've heard it all before. Tell me something new."

"I wish I could. I truly wish I could, Caleb." His voice was a mixture of care and hope.

"Hey," Caleb squeezed his shoulder. It's not your fault, Doc."

Dick Webster nodded solemnly. "Are you sticking to the macrobiotic diet?"

"C'mon. You know me better than that — I don't eat anything that can look back at me."

"Did you tell your new friend yet?"

"No. But I will as soon as the time is right."

"Here," the doctor said, reaching into the pocket of his lab coat, "you might need these."

Caleb opened his hand as the doctor placed a plastic container of three gold-foiled prophylactics. "Use them."

A lump caught in Caleb's throat. "Thanks, but I think my days of doing *that* are over ... Poor Buddy, he probably thinks I'm queer."

Dick Webster tried to laugh. "What's that supposed to mean?"

"We've been dating for a couple of weeks now, and I haven't touched him. As far as he knows, my house doesn't even have a bedroom."

"You can have safe sex — you know that. But tell him first. If he's half as nice as you've been telling me, he'll understand." Even as he spoke, the doctor wondered if Caleb's friend *would* understand. It was a combat zone out there, with families turning against their own.

"I wonder? I kind of hate to spoil things. He may be my last contact with a relationship."

"Nonsense. Tell him. Tell him to come and see me if he wants. We can all discuss it together."

Caleb stood and buttoned his shirt. He took a deep breath. "I'm having lunch with him today. I might as well get it over with."

Dick Webster patted him on the shoulder. "Call if you need me."

"I will, Doc."

Dick Webster fixed a plastic smile across his lips as Caleb exited. Then he closed the door to his office and returned to his desk. Then he buried his face in his hands and tried to block out the reality of the world.

"Is something wrong, Caleb?" Buddy asked over lunch at Casita's, a Mexican restaurant in Silverlake.

Caleb smiled wanly. "Pensive is all. How's the *molé*?"

Buddy picked his fork at the chicken covered in a thick chocolate sauce. It was hot. Spicy hot. So hot it made him sweat. He gulped a peach margarita. "Okay."

"How long have we been seeing each other, now?"

Buddy perked up. He'd been counting the minutes.

"Fifteen days ... I think." He didn't want to appear too eager.

"And, don't you think it's kind of peculiar that ... Well, that we haven't made love?"

Buddy studied the handsome blond face and blue eyes. "I've thought about it. Sure."

"And?"

"I like just being with you, Caleb."

"And I like being with you, too." He reached across the table and touched Buddy's hand. "But, there's a reason why we haven't made love."

Doubt pulled up along side Buddy's mind and threw on the emergency brakes. "Is it me, Caleb? You know, I won't always look like *this*. I've been going to the gym religiously. I'm starting to build up slowly but surely."

"It's not you, Buddy. I like you just the way you are."

Doubt pulled out and relief pulled in behind it. "I think it's better if we get to know each other first before jumping into bed. I'm happy just spending time with you."

Caleb studied the freckled man-child face as if each freckle had to be individually greeted. Buddy was so innocent. He didn't deserve this. Maybe they had just met at the wrong time in their lives.

"What is it, Caleb? Don't you want to see me anymore?"

"It's not that. I wish it was that simple."

"Then, what is it? You can tell me. I want to know everything about you."

"I have *AIDS*, Buddy." Caleb's voice was low and solemn.

Buddy's face fell into his chicken molé. He was stunned. "That's not funny, Caleb."

"I know. Unfortunately, it's true."

The color drained from Buddy's face. "I'm going to be sick!"

Downstairs in the restroom, Buddy leaned over the sink and splashed water on his face. He felt hot and unsteady.

As he reached for the paper towels to dry himself, a piece of graffiti on the restroom wall caught his attention. The crudely scribbled tenet slapped him across the face:

*AIDS = RECTAL ROULETTE!!*

He reached the porcelain just in time to feel his lunch leave his stomach.

# 31. Mazola Profundus

Working up a sweat, Scout attacked it with the savage grace of a jackhammer on butterfly wings.

Maizie lobbed him with a floury hand. "Hey, I said to whip it — not *beat* it to death!" She was attempting to teach him the art of baking a cake from scratch.

"Phew!" Wiping his forearm across his forehead, he continued creaming the butter with less vigor.

"Okay. That's good. Now, did you separate the eggs?"

"Yeah."

"*Well?*"

"Where are the eggs?"

"I put one in the living room and one in Jesse's bedroom."

Maizie's eyes rolled back in her head. "That's *not* what I meant by separate!" She shook her head. "Go and get them."

He retrieved them as ordered, and they continued.

"Now, fold them into the batter."

This was trickier than he expected. "Girl, how in hell do you *fold* an egg?"

"Oh, don't be so literal." She cracked the eggs and poured them into the bowl, nudging him with her elbow. "*That's* how!"

"Shoot, why didn't you say so?"

"I did." She then spooned in some brown sugar, cinnamon, a dash of nutmeg and vanilla. "It's almost ready. Did you preheat the oven?"

This was too easy. It must have been a trick question. "I turned it on, if that's what you mean."

"That's what I mean."

Just then, Jesse walked in and helped himself to a cup of coffee. Peering over their shoulders, he tried to dip his finger into the brown, speckled batter, but Maizie swatted him.

"I hope it tastes better than it looks."

"You hush," she winked. "Did you put Jackson to bed?"

He nodded, then stretched. "If I have to read *The Cat in the Hat* one more time, you'll have to have me committed."

She grinned knowingly, then slapped Scout's arm with her spatula. "Why don't you write him some new stories for Jackson?"

He backed off. "If you hit me one more time..."

"You'll what?"

He yanked the spatula from her hand. "I don't know, but it won't be pretty. Now, open that oven door or you'll be wearing this home tonight!"

The kitchen smelled of sugar and spice and everything nice.

"Get over here and sit down!" Maizie ordered.

Gently, Scout closed the oven door.

"If you don't stop looking at that cake, it's going to turn out flatter than a pancake. And take off that silly apron!"

He fluttered his hands beneath the ruffles. "No. I feel just like Donna Reed in this thing."

Maizie nudged Jesse, tapping her index finger to her temple. "That one's nuttier than a fruitcake."

Donna Reed executed a perfect pirouette in the middle of the kitchen floor. "Shoot, you're just jealous because it looks better on me than it ever did on you."

"You've definitely got your hands full with that one, Jesse." Maizie snickered.

Finally, Scout joined them at the kitchen table. He looked at Maizie pensively. "What exactly *do* you think of us?"

"I'm no bigot if that's what you're getting at." She got up and refilled everyone's cup. "My dear old mother used to tell us that God is colorblind." She returned the coffee pot to the stove. "I imagine He feels the same way about sex, too."

Scout guffawed. "Tell that to Pat Robertson."

She shook her head and sat back down. "All those religious zealots like Robertson and Falwell have taken Jesus hostage, and are holding him for ransom." She sipped her coffee. "'Whoever undertakes to set himself up in the field of Truth and Knowledge is shipwrecked by the laughter of gods.'"

Scout was a sucker for homilies. "Did your mama tell you that?"

"Einstein," Jesse injected. Scout wasn't used to her yet, but Maizie was a constant source of enlightenment to him.

"Well," Scout added, not one to be outdone, "my mama used to say, 'The Lord moves in mighty mysterious ways that we may not comprehend, but it's not up to us to ask or question why He does things one way or the other. Why He does things this way or that way.'"

Maizie nodded, listening intently.

Jesse had a suspicion something was afoot.

"Mama said," he continued, "'His ways are beyond our knowing — beyond the ken of human understanding — so just mind your own fuckin' business!'"

Maizie howled. "You devil," she laughed, rocking the table.

"Calm down, girl. You'll make my cake fall."

She wiped a tear from her eye. "Milo used to say, '*Chacun à son goût* — to each his own.'"

"Who's Milo?" Scout asked.

"Milo was my third husband — a New Orleans quadroon, with eyes bluer than a summer day." Her eyes twinkled in remembrance of things past.

Scout was impressed.

"Milo taught me a lot of things. And, as far as you two are concerned, all I see in this house is love. And folks making love makes more sense to me than folks making bombs that'll flambè the world."

It was overt simplicity, but common sense usually was.

"If I know my Bible, Jesus said, 'Where two or more are gathered in my name, there shall I be to bless.' And Jesus didn't qualify it, either. Two or more, and that's what you and Jesse are."

"Amen!" Scout smiled.

"Now, get that cake out of the oven before it turns into charcoal."

Hurriedly, he rescued his first cake as Maizie began pulling ingredients from the cupboards for frosting. "Child, this cake is going to sit up and talk!"


# 32. Night of the Living Dead

The chairs had been specially ordered from Italy — contraptions of black leather and gun-metal chrome that looked less comfortable than they actually were.

A luxurious handwoven rug from the People's Republic of China bathed the floor in deep Oriental splendor.

Sparkling mineral water and herb tea were set up beneath a Broadway poster of *Evita*.

The waiting room looked like a window in one of the shops along Designer's Row.

Buddy was reading a copy of *Per Lui*, when his name was called.

"Buddy Dove?"

He looked up into the matinee idol face of Dr. Dick Webster.

"Sorry to keep you waiting," he smiled, leading the way into the seclusion of his inner office. "Please have a seat."

Buddy felt like an errant schoolboy confronting the principal.

"I'm glad Caleb asked you to come and see me. I don't know if I can be of any help, but I'll be glad to answer any questions you have."

Buddy looked pallid. He tried to be calm and grownup, even though the earth seemed like it might give out beneath his feet at any moment. "Is Caleb going to be all right?"

The doctor was touched. He expected Buddy's first question to be about himself. A question like, how is this going to affect me? Am I safe? What should I do? Instead, his first concern was about Caleb. Nevertheless, Dick Webster believed in speaking the truth. "No, he's not, Buddy." He didn't want to bludgeon the young blond with the ugly facts, but those were the only facts available.

"He's going to ... *die?*"

The doctor nodded.

"What can I do?"

"If you want to help, you can be there for him. Respond to his emotions. Laugh when he laughs. Cry when he cries. Touch. Caress. Be prepared for Caleb to get angry with you for no obvious reason." The doctor paused. "Buddy, there's still time for you to get out of this. I know you haven't known Caleb very long. In a situation like yours, you can't really be expected to..."

Buddy cut him off. "I have no intention of abandoning him."

"Good. I just wanted to let you know what you're letting yourself in for. I'm afraid you're all Caleb has at this point."

Buddy looked shocked. "What about his family?"

"They've turned their back on him. I believe they've been giving him financial assistance since he lost his house, but no moral support. They made it perfectly clear to him that they do not want him home when ... At a time when he'll need them the most."

"His own family? How can they do that?"

The doctor didn't know how to answer. Unfortunately, it was another sad fact. One in a list of many.

Buddy spoke as if by rote. "How long..."

"Six weeks. Six months. A year..."

"But he's healthier than I am."

"He *seems* healthy, Buddy, but I can't tell you how long it will last before he becomes susceptible to something else. People die of complications — the myriad infections that assault the immune system until it finally weakens and breaks down altogether."

Buddy turned a whiter shade of pale.

A rabid Pentecostalist, foaming at the brain, decried the disease as a Gay Plague.

Jesse and Scout were glued to the Phil Donahue show when Buddy walked in. Scout was seeing red. "If I had a gun, I'd put this sucker out of his misery!"

Buddy walked lethargically to the sofa. Phil Donahue was delivering his best Alan Alda consciousness routine, but the holy roller wasn't buying it. He had a direct hotline to God.

Scout glanced at him, motioning him to sit down. "Man, I thought I'd seen everything, but this is a genuine *Ripley's Believe It Or Not!* An *asshole* talks! This fool makes the Ayatollah Khomeini look like E.T. They must make these fools take illiteracy tests before they ordain them. If they had their way we'd all be in cages."

"I thought the *Bible* said, 'Judge not, lest ye be judged,'" Jesse added.

Buddy's face was a blank. "What's it all about?"

"*AIDS,*" Scout replied. "I'm going to call in and tell that talking asshole what I think about him *and* his mama *and* the mule the bitch rode in on!"

Buddy turned from the television screen and walked to his bedroom like a zombie in a George Romero movie.

Jesse turned to Scout. "What's wrong with him?"

He shook his head. "I don't know, but he looks like he's lost his best friend."

## 33. Someday We'll Be Together

Nash was darker than a Boston baked bean, giving his tan the ultimate exposure. Shirtless and in jeans, he was busy packing up the belongings of his bedroom when Scout entered in one of the Hawaiian-print shirts he'd brought back for his landlocked ex-housemates.

Scout was on the attack. "You *can't* be serious?"

"Just hand me that box over there," Nash replied, "and, I am serious."

Scout handed him the box then sat on the bed, beneath a drooling Morris Louis lithograph. "I can't believe it. You're back from Hawaii one day, and the next thing I know you're moving out — with *him!*"

"Believe it. Dan was like another man in Hawaii. He loosened up, Scout. It was great."

"Yeah, but you're not *in* Hawaii, now. You're back in Boys' Town, back in the big closet Dan calls home."

Nash stopped packing for a moment and stared at him. "I thought you'd be happy for me. Happy that I've finally settled into a relationship."

"I am. But I know you, Nash. The reason you've never had a relationship before is because they have a way of interfering with your *other* relationships."

"Are you calling me a tramp?"

"Well, if the shoe fits. . ."

"Come on. It'll be more room for you and Buddy. I'll still be paying rent. You won't be hurt for money. My bed will still be here."

"But, you just can't!"

"Why?"

Scout thought for a moment. "It'd be like breaking up the Supremes. We're a trio, here. Who's going to sing lead? It won't be the same."

Nash embraced him. "You're nuts."

Scout was encased in wrap-around muscle. "If *I'm* nuts, why are you still going to pay rent?"

"Call it insurance."

"I will. *Casualty* insurance!"


"What's wrong with you?" Maizie asked as Scout entered the back door of Jesse's house. She was sitting at the kitchen table with Jesse, drinking coffee.

"Diana Ross has moved in with Dan Carlton." He helped himself to some coffee.

"What?"

Jesse spoke for Scout. "Nash is moving in with Dan."

Maizie's forehead wrinkled. "What's that got to do with Diana Ross?"

Scout stared at her. "The bitch has gone solo — after all these years together. We were a team."

"Buddy's still there, isn't he?"

"Oh, he's there *physically*. Mentally, I'm not too sure. The mood he's been in lately, I wouldn't be at all surprised if he finally moves back to Indiana."

Jesse motioned him to sit with them. "You've still got me and Maizie and Jackson."

"I know, but Nash and I grew up together. I always thought we'd be together until the end. You know, two old queens reminiscing about their glory days, living off social security and canned dog food."

Maizie contorted her face. "That's disgusting."

"Ain't it though. I give *that* relationship a month." He paused dramatically. "Nash knows you can't hurry love. You just have to wait. No matter how long it takes, you can't hurry love."

Maizie eyeballed Jesse. "Give me a break!"

Jesse grinned. "Maybe Nash hears a symphony."

"Maybe it's just an itchin' in his heart," Scout added.

"Or they've just been bitten by the love bug."

"Doesn't he know that boy he loves is just a Romeo?"

"Maybe he's grown impatient for a love he can call his own."

Maizie stood up, feet apart, one hand on her waist, one hand up, arm extended. "*Stop* — in the name of love!"

Jesse and Scout howled.

# 34. Blond on Blond

Buddy didn't smoke cigarettes, but if he did, he would have leaned languidly over Caleb's moist body for a post-coital puff. He was floating on a futon cloud of sweaty whooping cranes and bonsai trees enswirled in sweeping waves of pastel blues and pinks.

His relationship had finally been consummated via what seemed to be the Superbowl of Safe Sex. He had been drop-kicked through the goal posts of love to score a winning touchdown. The thrill of victory had never been so sweet or so safe. As his toes slowly uncurled and his endocrine system's last hurrah faded into the ethers, Buddy knew that it was at long last love.

"I don't know about you," Caleb panted, "but I think I just had a religious experience."

Buddy smiled. He had been turned inside out and back again. He looked through a cyclone of yellow straw at Caleb's naked body. It appeared invincible.

"I love you," Buddy murmured.

Caleb's eyes consumed the freckled man-child face. "I love you, too."

Caleb, who avoided hard liquor with the same intensity that a wino sought out a bottle of cheap wine, celebrated the evening with a double margarita at *El Coyote*.

"Here's to life," he smiled, clinking his glass against Buddy's. "If it ain't one thing, it's another."

Buddy forced a smile. "To life."

Instantly, Caleb detected that all was not well in the house of Buddy. "You don't sound like you mean it."

Buddy shrugged. "I do. It's just. . ."

Caleb placed his drink on the table. "Listen, I think it's time we laid down some ground rules."

"Ground rules?"

He nodded. "We've got to make the best of what time we have together now, Buddy. If you're not up to it, we'd better call it quits now."

"No, Caleb. No."

"Then, let's face the facts once and for all. If I can deal with this, you've got to learn to deal with it, too. It's that simple. And if you can't deal with it, you'd better deal yourself out right now."

A tear fell down Buddy's cheek into his margarita. "Deal me in," he sniffled.

"Come on. No backsliding. No feeling sorry for yourself. No remorse. We're going to fight this thing all the way, okay?"

"Okay."

Caleb nudged him lightly on the chin with his knuckles. "Let's order."

Over Mexican coffee and dessert, Caleb dropped the final bomb. Buddy was on his second flan when it detonated.

"There's something else," Caleb said reluctantly. "I think we should have a final game plan. A password or something that'll tell you when to leave."

"Leave?" Buddy had started to signal a passing waitress in a hoop skirt and an off-the-shoulder blouse, with eyelashes thick as tarantula legs and bright maraschino lips. She looked like a road company Scarlett O'Hara.

"Listen to me, Buddy."

He turned his attention back to the handsome blond face on the other side of the table. Scarlett whizzed past with a tray of frozen margaritas, skirts rustling. "I'm listening."

"Towards the end," Caleb said, brushing back a shock of pale blond hair from his forehead, "when I'm debilitated and no longer myself, I want you to leave. Go somewhere. Take a little trip. I have some money put aside just for you."

Buddy couldn't believe what he was hearing. Caleb was talking quietly and rationally about his own demise.

"So, when this catch phase is spoken, that'll be your clue to get away ... I don't want you to remember me *that* way. I want you to remember me the way I am *tonight*. Will you do that one final thing for me when the time comes?"

Buddy's lower lip trembled slightly. He nodded.

"Good." Caleb immediately brightened. "Have you ever seen Charles Pierce? I bought tickets for his show. He's going to be in town soon. I think we could use the laughs."

Buddy's face was a mask of wistfulness. He could definitely use some laughs.

# 35. Praise the Lord

He carried on like a rabid banshee on an amphetamine high after signing the registered letter from the postman, who happened to be a woman.

Scout had an innate feeling this was it. He ripped the envelope open.

"Thank you, Jesus! Thank you, Jesus!! ThankyouJesus!!!"

Assulting the contents of the letter with a series of passionate kisses, he dashed out the back door and down the street, running as if his life depended on it; as if a swarm of hostile killer bees had a contract on him.

A man in jeans and powder-blue LaCoste turned to his companion as Scout wailed past them towards Boys' Town.

"Now that's what I call a screaming queen!"

The other man nodded. "He was kinda cute, though."

The first man rolled his eyes. "If you're into the encyclopedic look!"

Jesse's foot practically went through the floorboard as the truck screeched to an abrupt halt. Two cars behind him swerved and burned rubber in an ominous echo.

"Asshole!" he yelled, but the figure darting across the intersection kept right on moving. He shook his head in disgust until he recognized the object of his contempt. "Jesus, it's Scout!"

Maizie saw him galloping up the sidewalk and ran from the house. Her female intuition told her that something had happened, but it didn't tell her what. He looked like a wild man.

Scout grabbed her by the waist and twirled like Stevie Nicks.

She must have realized it was nothing drastic, because she joined right in in a swirl of centrifugal force. Moments later, their grasp breaking, they flew across the yard onto their asses.

Jesse peeled rubber up the street to his house, roaring into the driveway. He jumped from the truck ready to kill, but Maizie and Scout were laughing like a calliope.

"What in hell is going on? I practically ran your ass over back there."

Scout jumped to his feet and leaped at him.

Jesse caught him, but the flying weight sent them both to the ground. Scout kissed him wildly. "We hit the fucking motherlode, Jesse. We're rich!"

Maizie ran to their side. "What'd you say?"

Scout waved the check in their faces. "*Look!*"

Jesse snatched the check from his hand. It was a cashier's check for $25,000, made out in Scout's name. He was stunned.

Maizie quickly snatched the check from him. "Sweet baby Jesus!" Her hands clutched her heart.

"Sweetness had nothing to do with it." Scout was delirious. "Can you believe it?"

Maizie stared at it again. "$25,000!" She looked like she was going to pee in her panties. "Where'd you get it?"

"*I won!!* Jesus Great God A'Mighty — *I won!!*"

"Won what, child?"

"The Bake N' Biscuit Sweepstakes!"

Maizie really looked confused. "But you can't even cook!"

"No, but I can write my name and address and that's exactly what I did. For a month. A thousand times!"

Everyone grinned from ear to ear. Scout hugged and kissed them both. "You're lookin' at one mighty happy queer!"

Jesse was ecstatic. "Make that *two* happy queers!"

"Make that two happy queers and one stunned black woman!"

They fell to the grass in hysterics, proving that money *can* buy happiness.

"What are you going to do with it?" Jesse laughed.

Scout brushed himself off. "Buy Ted and Justine's house if it's still for sale."

"What?" Jesse got to his feet.

"Right on!" Maizie squealed.

"Let's go," Scout yelled, jumping inside the truck's cab, "time's a-waistin'. Throw the mothafuka in gear and make tracks!"

"Where are we going?"

"To the GO FOR IT Realty Company. This check is the down payment on our new home. Now, move this sucker!"

They were already standing outside the house when the real-tor, a svelte lipstick lesbian with a shock of curly auburn hair, pulled her blood-red Jeep into the driveway.

"Welcome home," she smiled, clearly pleased that her new clients were able to buy what was evidently their dream house. It was one of the fastest deals she had ever closed. "Of course," she winced, "it needs a little work. The former owners were . . . a bit wierd."

"That's an understatement," Jesse grinned.

"Oh, you knew them. Well, for the price, I don't think you can beat it, despite the elbow grease it's going to need to get it into shape."

"We've got plenty of that," Scout smiled.

"Well, then, I'll just leave the keys with you and meet you back at my office."

# 36. There's No Place Like Home

Nash stopped by the house on the way to work after receiving Scout's telephone call. When he got there, he sensed something was cooking; luckily it wasn't in the kitchen.

Whatever it was, Scout was acting like Doug Henning at a magician's convention.

"So, what's the scoop?" he asked, entering his old abode.

"Yeah, Scout," Buddy prodded.

Jesse was the only one semi-composed, but a twinkle in his eyes said he was itching for Scout to talk, too.

Then, Maizie, dressed in a striking spaghetti-strap cocktail dress; turquoise and spangled, cut low in the front and high above the knees, swept into the living room hustling a tray of canapes. Scout was right behind her with a bottle of champagne.

"Doesn't she look great?" he beamed.

Maizie did a quick pirouette. "I knew if I hung on to this sucker, it'd come back in style — and, I was *right!*"

"Come on, Scout," Nash egged, "what's this all about?"

"Better tell them," Jesse laughed, "or Nash is going to bring out the Jaws of Life and rip it out of you."

"Wait," Maizie yelled, always one for propriety. "Pour the champagne first. We have to have a toast."

Nash followed Jesse into the kitchen and pulled out the fluted champagne glasses from the cupboards.

"What's going on around here?" he asked, grabbing Jesse's arm. "Did you get Scout pregnant, or what?"

Nash was ecstatic. "All right!" he yahooed. "Damn, and I thought all that sweepstakes jazz was a big hoax."

Buddy couldn't believe his ears.

"Well, it finally paid off," Nash laughed, lifting Scout with a rib-crushing bear hug.

"What finally paid off?" Maizie asked, draining her fluted glass, and quickly pouring herself another.

"Scout's . . . *indefatigable* faith in hitting the jackpot. He's been entering every sweepstakes known to the free world for years. When we were in college, he almost dropped out of school because he received a notice in the mail that said he *may* have already won the Reader's Digest Sweepstakes."

"Shoot, how was I to know they mailed those notices out by the thousands?" Scout countered.

Jesse gave his main man a reassuring sqeeze.

"Hey," Nash added, "where is it? The house, I mean?"

"Right here in Boys' Town. Ted and Justine's old place. Can you believe it?"

"I knew there had to be a reasonable explanation for *that* friendship."

"We'll all go over tomorrow and start drawing up the plans. Jesse and I will take the downstairs, and you and Buddy can have the upstairs."

Nash looked at everyone in the room until his eyes met up with Scout's. "Excuse me, but in case you've forgotten, I'm living with Dan Carlton, now."

Scout shrugged. "Oh, yeah. Well, we'll fix up a room for you anyway. Just in case."

"Just in case of what?"

"Just in case you have to file a claim on your insurance."

Jesse looked at him quizzically. "Insurance?"

Scout adjusted his glasses, then started toward the champagne for a refill, calling over his shoulder. "Casualty Insurance."

"Up yours!" Nash retorted. "Everything's going to work out fine."

"I'll drink to that," Maizie saluted, holding her glass in the air a little too vigorously.

"That sentiment, I'm afraid, is debatable. Have you seen the latest issue of *Hollywood Tattletales?*"

"No. Why?"

"I think Dan Carlton is going to be interested in it. There's a little item about the both of you."

Nash's eyes widened. "Uh-oh."

"It seems the cat was caught with canary feathers *alllll* over it's mouth," Scout needled. "You'd better stop off at a hardware store and get a hammer on your way home from work tonight."

"Why?"

"Well, you're going to need something to get him out of that closet he lives in."

# 37. What's Love Got to Do With It?

After Nash punched in the correct numbers for the electronic security system that guarded Dan Carlton's mini-fortress, he tiptoed into the kitchen.

Outside it should have been pitch black, but the pool lights were on; so was the jacuzzi. Looking out the kitchen window, he saw that Dan was still up.

"What are you doing up this late?" he asked, walking up to the steaming jacuzzi.

Dan was three sheets to the wind. His speech was slurred. "Have you seen this rag?"

Nash glanced down at the wet copy of *Hollywood Tattletales*, on the deck along side the jacuzzi. "Is this what's got you so paranoid? This piece of trash?" He picked it up and glanced through it. "Nobody pays attention to this crap."

Water bubbled about Dan's chest. He wasn't so sure; people

seemed to thrive on gossip. "Did you read it? I should sue the rotten bastards."

Nash took it into the kitchen where it was light. He quickly turned the cover over to a crudely typed page of gossip. He rolled his eyes. Dan had highlighted it with a yellow marker: *Special Bulletin!! What local anchorman has the trots for one of Boys' Town's hottest gay bartenders? We won't tell, but they were spotted deplaning from Aloha Airlines, proud as peacocks. Hint! Hint! But that's not the real scoop. The real 'news' is that Mr. Emmy-winning Anchorman is supposed to be 'straight!!!' If he is, it'll be 'news' to his viewers. Then again, maybe it won't! Mr. Gay Bartender didn't look too surprised. Stay tuned. 'News' at 4!!!"*

Dan wobbled into the kitchen, robed and dripping.

Nash's eyes narrowed. "Big deal. It could be anyone."

"Hardly. The little pricks even named the 4 o'clock news."

"You don't blame *me* for this, do you?"

Dan sipped the remains of a cocktail, unwilling to meet Nash's eyes. Behind him a shooting star arched above the mountains of the *Hollywood* sign. Finally, he spoke. "I don't think we should see each other any more. At least, for a while." His voice was remote and emotionless, as if he were reporting the famine in Ethiopia.

"Well, that's going to be cute since we're both living in the same house. How do you propose we do that?"

Dan squelched a burp. "I think *that's* self-explanatory."

Nash's eyes turned scalpel sharp. He looked like he was about to perform open-face surgery with his bare hands. "Man, when are you going to face *what* you are?"

Dan's half-mast eyes widened to full staff. "I sure as hell don't need *you* to tell me *what* I am!"

"The hell you don't." Nash was steaming. "You don't give a damn about me. All you care about is your *career!*"

"You're damn right! My career will still be around long after you're gone. Do you think I want to be a *local* anchor all my life? I'm going *national*, and I'm not about to let everything I've worked for be destroyed by petty innuendo."

Nash headed for the door, turning back before his final exit. "Next time you want to get laid — try fucking your fucking career!"

*"But ya are, Blanche! But ya are!!"*

The Late Late Show kept Scout company as he packed the Fiestaware. Baby Jane Hudson was putting the screws to her invalid sister and enjoying every second of it.

Suddenly, Scout froze. His eyes darted to the front door as the dead bolt clicked. The hair on the back of his neck stood on end.

Slowly, the door opened.

He grabbed his heart. "Jesus, don't do that."

It was Nash. "What's wrong with you?"

"I thought it was Baby Jane Hudson. What are you doing here this late?"

"Don't ask, okay. Can I spend the night?"

"Of course you can. You can sleep in my room. Buddy's staying over at his boyfriend's tonight, and your room's all packed up."

"Buddy's got a boyfriend?"

"Yeah. We're all going to meet him tomorrow. So, what happened? You're not cheating on Dan *already*, are you?"

"That prick! It's over. *Finis. Kaput.*" He shook his head in disgust. "Man, he is such a..."

"Closet queen?"

Nash gritted his teeth. "Such a ... *sonofabitch!*"

"That was my second guess. So, what happened?"

"Nothing but Wham-Bang-Thank-You-Sam — don't let the door hit you in the ass! He never loved me. I was just another sexual object to him."

"You should be used to that by now," Scout grinned.

"Very funny. I never want to see that man again!"

Scout was jubilant. "Good. I hope she *suffocates!*"

# 38. Truffles

It boomed! The man's voice was deep and resounding, infused with the after effects of a double-martini and olive lunch (thrice served).

He was addressing a companion who, bibulously speaking, had had one too many and was doing his best to place a folded ten dollar gratuity on the white plastic tray Buddy had placed on their table.

Stumbling from their chairs, one or the other inadvertently toppled a water glass, spilling $H_2O$ across the pressed linen tablecloth. Neither seemed disturbed by the aqueous faux pas, each possibly assuming the other had caused it, each deciding it was best left ignored. Besides, what's a little spilled water between friends?

"Have you been to the Safeway on Santa Monica, George?" the boomer boomed, continuing the conversation as he navigated an imperfect path through the encroaching tables of afternoon diners (a feat not easily executed under the influence of distilled Russian spuds — thrice served). His gait, swerving and unsteady, resembled an unchoreographed dance with gravity — gravity leading!

"Well, you *must* go, George," he bellowed. "I tell you, it's cruisier than the bars. I can't remember when I've ever seen so many *fruits* in the vegetable section!"

A pregnant woman, looking suspiciously like an incognito Bette Midler, cooed to her luncheon companion as the elderly gentlemen zigzagged past: "Girl, those turkeys are *plucked!*"

Scout and Jesse were laughing when Nash joined them beneath a red and blue Cinzano umbrella. "Did you see them, too?"

Jesse nodded. "How could you miss them?"

"Hey," Scout grinned, "who said, 'Candy is dandy, but liquor is quicker?'"

"Mamie Eisenhower?" Jesse guessed.

Nash shook his head. "Wrong. It was either Pat Nixon or Betty Ford."

"You guys are too cold," Scout admonished. "Anyway, you're both wrong. I remember now. It was Ogden Nash."

Nash deadpanned him. "Well, where do you think *he* got it?"

Seconds later, their attention was diverted toward Buddy and a handsome blond in a Perry Ellis sport coat and jeans, maneuvering their way through the maze of tables and scurrying busboys. Few heads turned, but the majority of seasoned eyes, who had seen everything from punk rockers to Oscar winners, discreetly shifted their eyes to peripheral vision.

Everyone at the table stood up.

"Jesus, I thought those two old farts would never leave," Buddy smiled. "Everybody, this is Caleb."

The men introduced themselves, each one shaking Caleb's hand, then sat back down.

Scout clearly looked pleased at Buddy's newfound friend.

Nash was undressing him with his eyes. "So, what exactly do you do, Caleb?"

"I practiced law once. I'm afraid I'm between jobs at the moment."

Scout's eyes lit up, like a mother welcoming her potential son-in-law. Even if he wasn't employed, it was a good catch for Buddy. "Well, Caleb, welcome to the group. I hope it's a long and prosperous friendship."

Buddy winced.

"So do I," Caleb replied, squeezing Buddy's thigh beneath the table. "So do I."

# 39. There's No Place Like Home

Maizie took one look at the inside of Ted and Justine's old home, exclaiming: "Child, black is beautiful, but *not* on the walls!"

In the following weeks, Dracula-black walls disappeared behind Pacific Cowhide Suede. Fifties fixtures gave way to multiple track lighting and dimmer switches. Mini blinds were ordered. Furniture was moved in, arranged and rearranged until everyone was satisfied. Earth tones were prevalent as were the verdant hues of dracaenas and schleffleras. By the time the Fiestaware was unpacked and hit the cupboards, it was beginning to look like home.

With the exception of one stairway, allowing access between the upstairs and downstairs quarters, the renovations on Queens Range were underway.

In his heart of hearts, Scout deYoung was finally getting the family he couldn't genetically reproduce with the one person he loved best in the world, who just happened to be another man.

Even though the household knew Scout's culinary knowledge wouldn't have filled the back panel of a Stouffer's box, it was, nevertheless, the downstairs kitchen that became the residents' weekend hangout.

Cooking might have been an enigma to him, despite Maizie's myriad attempts at teaching him otherwise, but brewing from the bean was second nature to him. Although Jesse claimed Scout's coffee had sprouted new hairs on his chest and was so strong NASA could have used it for rocket fuel, he did, all in all, give good coffee.

Dressed in everyday drag — blue cord painter pants, scuffed white leather Nikes and a long-sleeved shirt rolled up at the elbows — Scout was trying his best to wake up. The Arabica brew Mr. Coffee was sending out wafted about the house like an olfactory alarm clock, but he was still on snooze control.

Buddy came down first, dressed in a seafoam green polo shirt and shorts.

Scout stared at him through groggy eyes. "Well, if it isn't Doris Day's son." There were times when Buddy looked like a walking advertisement for Wonder Bread.

"Morning," he replied, pouring himself a cup of coffee. "Where's Jesse?"

"He took Jackson to the lumberyard to buy some wood for Scooter's doghouse."

"Jackson got a dog?"

"Sort of. Only nobody can see him except Jackson."

"Why?"

"Because Scooter's *invisible*. Isn't Nash coming down?"

Buddy shrugged; sipped his coffee. "He's not alone."

"*Again!*" Scout shook his head. "Did you see that fireman he brought home the other night? He made Sylvester Stallone look like Pee-Wee Herman."

"He certainly is resilient."

"I'll say. It sounded like a three-alarm fire up there. I guess firemen can start fires as well as put them out."

Buddy grinned.

"So, kiddo, where's Caleb? You two are getting pretty tight, aren't you? Why don't you tell your Auntie Scout all about it." His eyebrows did little calisthenics above his eyes. "It's pretty serious, isn't it?"

Buddy's grin backflipped to an upside-down Happy Face. "It's *very* serious."

"Good." Scout patted his hand. "Now, didn't I tell you these things take time? I like Caleb. I think he's just what the doctor ordered."

Buddy's face crumpled. "Scout..."

"Hey, what's wrong?"

He got up and got a paper towel to dry his tears. "It's Caleb. He's..."

"He's what?"

"He's going ... to die."

"I don't believe it." A picture of the healthy blond flashed through Scout's brain. "What makes you say a thing like that?"

A lump the size of an onion caught in Buddy's throat. "He's got AIDS, Scout."

Scout fell back in his chair as if he'd had the wind knocked out of him. "Jesus!"

# 40. People's Parties

Four weeks had passed since Nash had spoken to Dan Carlton. He wanted to call, but his male pride, heavier than a barbell on a forced-rep, wouldn't allow it.

Groveling wasn't in his repertoire of socially acceptable behavior. Dan would have to call him.

In the interim, a waiter, named Andy, from Truffles, invited him to a party being given by a wealthy gay attorney. The address was in Beverly Hills, a hop, skip and a jump from Boys' Town.

Dress was casual, Andy had told him, which in Southern California meant cheap chic — anything from leather tuxes to the old standby denim and flannel. Nash decided on a pair of charcoal Chereskin cords and an indigo Basic Elements polo sweater.

Andy looked like the Mad Hatter behind the wheel of his white VW Rabbit convertible.

"Is this the place?" Nash asked, as Andy screeched into a circular red brick driveway. Huge columns framed the mansion. It looked like Tara's little sister, Beverly Hills style. Off to the side, between a landscape of Mercedeses and BMWs, was a singular, pristine Rolls-Royce.

Andy fished in the pocket of his paisley shirt, producing a Lilliputian-sized vial with a connecting silver spoon. He elbowed Nash. "It's the *real* thing! Uncut, too!"

"Hmmm, just the way I like my men," Nash acquiesced without hesitation.

When they reached the front doors they were both sniffling cheerfully.

"No matter where you go," Nash said, "there you are."

"Huh?"

"Buckeroo Banzai," he winked, as the front doors opened to a sea of glossy passport smiles.

The interior of the mansion was extreme opulence, à la *Lifestyles of the Rich and Famous*. Even the guests seemed like an integral part of the decor.

The living room opened on to a patio, and both were swimming with well-built, male-model types. It looked like the reception room for *GQ*. Andy's eyes ignited like torches.

"This must be what gay heaven looks like," he beamed.

Nash thought it looked more like an Allan Carr fantasy.

Andy nudged him. "I'm going to *powder* my nose. Want another toot?"

"Later. I need a drink first."

They took off in opposite directions.

Nash settled next to a native girl by Gauguin. It appeared to be the *real* thing.

"Nice party." The man addressing him was wearing baggy Yohji Yamamoto pants, a bleached linen t-shirt and an oversized pastel blue jacket. White symmetrical teeth flashed confidently beneath a black moustache.

"Great," Nash lied. It was like being at a mannequin's convention.

The man scanned the crowd. "Do you really think so?" His voice was a sexy basso.

"Well..."

"By the way, I'm Dick Webster."

"Nash Aquilon." He shook the man's hand firmly. Somehow, he looked familiar. "Say, have we met before?"

"I would have remembered if we had. Do you read *The Advocate*, by any chance?"

"Occasionally."

"Maybe you've seen my ad. Dr. Dick Webster, Gay M.D."

Nash's face broke into a broad smile. "Hey, you're the one that was in *Playgirl*."

He stood accused. "You've got a good memory — that was quite a few years ago. I'm afraid it was a momentary lapse of character on my part."

"I thought you looked familiar. I rarely forget a..."

"Face?"

Nash's libido was showing. "Close. You know, you're *very* photogenic," he joked. "So, you're the one."

"I'm the one what?"

"That discovered a vaccine for *ugly*. Jesus, I never thought I'd OD on classically chiseled features. Look, there's not a sorry face in the crowd."

The doctor was looking. "You can say that again," he replied, doing a quick topographical survey of Nash's body.

Glaciers were melting.

"Come on, Nash," Andy protested. "The ice is just starting to break. You can't go now. Stick around."

"You can take care of yourself," Nash assured him. Andy had consumed so much coke he looked like he was wired for video. "Besides, look over there."

Andy followed his eyes. "Hey, that's whatshisname — the gay doctor."

"Ain't it though."

Andy looked back and forth between them. "You mean ...

you two ... You're leaving with him?"

"Fast thinking, Sherlock."

He punched Nash's shoulder. "Hey, I hear he's got a great *stethoscope!*"

"Right again."

Andy grabbed Nash's arm before he could get away. "Ask him if he's got medical insurance on that thing!"

## 41. Strangers in the Night

He slammed the telephone receiver down.

Dan Carlton was still reeling from his telephone conversation with Scout: Nash was out! Nash was at a party! I'll tell him you called! Click!

His second telephone call soon canceled out the icy reception of the first. Midnight Escorts would soon see to that, discretion being the better part of sex for hire.

It was bigger than a six-shooter; larger than a Magnum; closer to that long, sleek rifle known as a Winchester Special. The midnight cowboy entering Dan Carlton's front door packed an appendage like Trigger's, holstered in denim and Marlboro chaps. He wore a Stetson, an embroidered calico shirt opened to the waist, a leather vest as mean as the grin on a hungry coyote, and a neckerchief tied above the heaviest set of pecs this side of Boys' Town. His handtooled cowboy boots were from the renown ranges of Neiman-Marcus, Beverly Hills.

Dan Carlton was salivating faster than Gene Autry could say, "Git along little dogie." He closed the door behind his midnight special, scouting the rugged terrain of the cowboy's denimed buttocks.

"I'm Clint," the cowboy smiled, tipping his hat. His Texas twang said he'd wagged more tails than a nest of rattlesnakes and ninety-nine percent of them had been about as appetizing as an armadillo's behind. Tonight there would be no trouble unloading his pistol. His client was a hunk. But his cordiality quickly shifted to the acumen of a true businessman. "Will this be cash or credit card?"

Dan quickly surrendered his American Express card to the cowboy.

"I like to get business out of the way first," Clint said blandly, "then we can concentrate on pleasure."

Dan began shedding his clothes. Midnight Escorts charged by the hour.

Across town it was a different story. No charge, and service with a smile.

The doctor was a smooth operator. Nash ended up at the doctor's house in a bedroom *pas de deux*. The bartender had no idea safe sex could be so much fun.

It was a little after the fact, but the doctor inquired just the same. "Do you have a lover?"

Nash exhaled a stream of smoke and snubbed his cigarette.

"Not exactly."

"Not exactly? What's *that* mean?"

"We've been ... *incommunicado*."

"Couldn't handle it, huh?"

"There were lots of things he couldn't handle. I happened to be one of them."

"Lucky for me. Whoever it was was a fool."

"One of us was, anyway."

"Did you love him?"

Nash rolled over on his side, facing the doctor. "Define *love*."

"That's a tough one. Let's see ... Love is a responsible act of nurturing and enhancing another person's life."

"I'll buy that."

"You can't buy it — it's free."

"Whatever you say."

"Well, did you love him?"

"I guess I was close. How about you? Do you have a lover?"

The doctor laughed. "If I did, you wouldn't be here. I'm the old-fashioned type."

Nash pinched his nipple. "I can't believe *you* don't have a lover. As good looking as you are."

"Hey! I didn't say I was the Virgin Queen!"

Nash chuckled. "Love is strange. There's so many variables and so few constants. That's why I stick to sex."

The doctor folded his hands behind his head, studying the ceiling. "My philosphy of love is that it's like riding a horse. If you get thrown, you've got to dust yourself off and get back on."

"Thank you, Dr. Ruth." He laughed out loud, not at the doctor, but at something that popped into his mind.

"What's so funny?"

"I was just thinking about my friend, Scout. He was born with moons in his eyes. Sometimes it takes him *years* to get back on the horse, but when he does, he invariably picks a winner."

"And you?"

He laughed again. "Scout says I have the resiliency of Boat & Deck paint. I've got a Teflon heart. I think my Y chromosomes are rabid."

"Lucky for you I'm a doctor."

"Am I? Scout says love is contagious, but that it's seldom fatal. He should know, too. He's been on the critical list enough times."

"And what do *you* think?"

"What do I think?" Nash shrugged his shoulders. "I think it's fun while it lasts."

"That's the trick, huh? Making it last."

"Yeah. You'd think there'd be a serum for it."

# 42. Quantum Reality

"What did Jane Pauley just say?" Maizie turned from preparing Jackson's lunch for preschool.

Jesse heard it, too, and hurried into the kitchen. His eyes darted to the mini-TV Maizie kept on the counter. "What'd she just say?"

Scout, who was sitting at the kitchen table, turned to them dumbfounded. "Rock Hudson's in Paris. He has AIDS."

"Good God!" Jesse gasped.

Maizie quickly said a silent prayer for the handsome movie star.

"And Buddy just asked me last night if Caleb could move in with us." Scout was still in a daze.

"What'd you tell him?" Maizie asked, stuffing a Ding Dong into Jackson's lunchbox.

"They're moving in this afternoon. Jesus, what have I done?"

"What's that suppose to mean?" Maizie's prejudice detector zoomed in on Scout's thought like radar. Her eyes narrowed.

"Caleb has AIDS."

"We know that. You told us the other night," she said, scrutinizing Scout like a microbe under a microscope.

"Well, obviously this is much more serious than any of us thought. We can't let him move in with us now."

"*Scout!*" Jesse was shocked. "Didn't you also tell us that Caleb's parents have ostracized him from his own family? The poor guy can't even go home."

"Jesse, we have a child in the house, not to mention the rest of us. Christ, what if he gave it to one of us!"

Maizie butted in. "That's just plain ignorance, Scout. He can't give it to us. Don't you read the papers? Don't you watch TV? You subscribe to *Time* and *Newsweek* — you ought to try reading them once in a while."

"Well, *excuse* me for being concerned!"

Maizie's hands were on her hips. "Concern is one thing — *stupidity* is another thing all together!"

"Are you calling me stupid?"

Maizie turned back to Jackson's lunch. "If the shoe fits."

"Damnit, don't make me the villain of this little melodrama."

"*Melodrama?*" Now, Jesse was riled. "This little melodrama, as you call it, is about life and death. I'm shocked, Scout. I thought I knew you better than that."

Scout felt his face turn hot.

"We all voted on this thing, and as far as I'm concerned, Caleb is moving in with us. I'm not turning *my* back on a friend," Jesse stated bluntly.

"Right on!" Maizie amened.

"A *friend!*" Scout said irritably. "We hardly know him!"

Maizie's eyes flashed with anger. "You're not only heartless, you're prejudiced *and* closed-minded! I thought your mama raised you better than that. Lord knows you're always talking about 'Mama said *this* — Mama said *that.*'"

Scout was too hurt to reply. Maizie had called his bluff, catching his ideology with its pants down around its principles. He was a fraud.

"And what about all the rhetoric, Scout?" Jesse added. "You're always espousing gay rights. What about Caleb's rights? And Buddy's rights, too? He's got a say-so about what goes on in this house as well as you do."

That did it. Even his lover was against him. Scout fled the room, but Maizie called after him, adding insult to injury. "And running away isn't going to change a thing!"

Scout's mama always said, "When the going gets tough, the tough go shoppin'." She also said that when a problem confronts you, you got two choices: fight it and make your life miserable or face it head-on and learn from it, and maybe grow a little in the process.

He thought about this as he cruised aimlessly through Boys' Town. Suddenly it hit him. His mama and Jesse and Maizie were right. It was one thing to talk about what was right, and another thing to act upon what was right.

He decided to act. The green Volvo headed down the boulevard toward Hollywood. His decision to *act* led him to the AID FOR AIDS PROJECT.

The young man typing at the front desk looked like he was about Buddy's age. He was preppy-looking, with short blond hair falling across his forehead in a boyish haircut. He wore a crisp Oxford shirt, a Cartier silk tie and a gold lambda tiepin. "Can I help you?" he asked professionally.

Scout hovered over the desk. "I'd like to talk to someone," he said quietly.

"About AIDS?"

He nodded.

"Let me see if anyone is available." Pressing a button, he buzzed someone in the next room. "Peter, there's someone out here that would like some information."

Seconds later a man appeared, about Scout's height and

build, in navy cords and a Navajo-patterned Ragg sweater. He had dark curly hair and wore glasses. "Hi, I'm Peter."

Scout shook his hand. "I'm Scout deYoung."

Peter looked him up and down, then adjusted his glasses perfunctorily. "Are you interested in volunteer work? We always need people to answer the AIDS Hotline or type. And then there's the Buddy Program."

Scout ad-libbed. "Actually, I'm just doing research . . . I'm a writer. I was hoping to get some facts."

"Well, I was about to leave." He checked his watch. "If you'd like, you're welcome to ride along with me and we could talk then. I'm afraid the *facts* are pretty ugly. Someone's been evicted from his home." He pushed back a cluster of black curls from his forehead. "The poor guy has lived there for ten years. He was fired from his job when they discovered he has AIDS, and now his landlord has locked him out of his apartment and thrown all of his belongings into the street. Can you *believe* that?"

"That's terrible." Scout hoped Peter wasn't telepathic. At that moment, he felt about three inches tall.

"Tell me about it. People are reacting in all the wrong ways. Reasoning is out and fear and ignorance is in. People have just got to be *educated!*" He glanced at the clock on the office wall. "Well, I guess I'd better get over there."

As they walked to Peter's car, he turned to Scout. "Did you hear about Rock Hudson?"

He nodded.

"Now maybe the government will get off their asses and do something about it!"

# 43. When the Saints Go Marching In

It was already dark when Scout returned home. The days were getting shorter; the nights longer. There was a sporadic chill to the night air. Pretty soon it would be time to get out his letterman jacket or the broad-shouldered Calvin Klein bomber jacket Noah had bought him that last Christmas before he died. A jacket he loved. The accentuated shoulders always made him feel just like Joan Crawford.

Jazz and laughter filtered downstairs from the direction of Nash's bedroom as Scout entered through the back door. His best friend's indefatigability at sex suddenly frightened him. Nash changed men like he changed his clothes, sending them out when they were soiled or finding new ones when the occasion called for it. He did more business than the local Fluff & Fold. Even if Nash's libido was permanent press, the dangerous implications of hit-and-run sex sent a chill up Scout's spine. After his discussion with Peter, it came down to one thing: No glove, no love. He hoped Nash was covered.

"Where've you been?" Jesse yawned, rubbing the sleep from his eyes after napping on the sofa.

Scout hadn't even noticed him standing in the doorway dividing the kitchen and living room. "Out," he replied gingerly.

Jesse stared at him. "Are you hungry? Maizie left a plate for you in the oven."

Avoiding his lover's eyes, Scout headed towards the stove, but Jesse beat him to it. "Sit down. I'll get it for you."

After bringing the plate to the kitchen table, Jesse sat down opposite Scout, studying his face. "Are you mad at me?"

Scout nodded quietly.

"We were pretty rough on you this morning. I apologize."

Scout shook his head, still not meeting Jesse's eyes. "I'm not mad at you," he sighed to his mashed potatoes. "I'm mad at myself."

"Well, don't be too hard on yourself."

"I can't help it. I looked the beast in the eye today, and it turned out *I* was the beast. It was pretty upsetting." He picked at his green beans. "I'm a fraud, Jesse."

"No you're not."

"I am. I'm ... lower than a gnat's ass. I'm a Janus-faced hypocrite ... I'm..."

"Hey, nobody's perfect." Jesse put his index finger under Scout's chin, tilting his face upward.

"I'm no better than that righteous right-wing Moral Majority moron that was on TV the other day. I don't deserve you."

Jesse snickered. "I didn't move in with you because I thought your mama was Mother Theresa or that you were St. Francis of A-sissy, Boys' Town chapter. Nobody is infallible, Scout. We're all just human beings."

"Maybe, but sometimes I feel if they did a brain scan on me, they'd come up empty."

"We all have those days when we feel like the inmates of the Asylum of Charenton and the Marquis de Sade seems to be directing our lives. I know you, Scout. You may have spoken hastily about Caleb, but after you've thought it through, you'll do the right thing. You always do. I'm sure of it."

"I hope you're right."

# 44. No Frills

Caleb stirred gently beneath the blankets.

Buddy followed the rhythm of his body, seeking the intimate coziness of warm flesh, clinging to his lover's body like human Glad Wrap. Even in the altered consciousness of half-sleep, he knew innately there was nothing quite like the communication of two naked, loving souls. He nuzzled against Caleb like a bear settling in for the winter.

Caleb murmured and rolled on top of him, burying his face between Buddy's shoulder and neck. "How would you like to see Mexico?"

Buddy groaned. "Who's at the Texaco?"

"*Texaco?* I said Mexico. Come on, let's be spontaneous. We can drive down this morning and camp out on the beach for a few days. Just the two of us. It'll be great."

Buddy's eyes fluttered open, although the look on his face said he was quite content right where he was, thank you.

"I mean it. Let's go right now. You'll love it."

"You're serious, huh?"

"Yeah. We can pitch a tent right under the stars."

Buddy leaned on his elbow, then scratched his haystack early-morning hairdo. "Right now?"

"Right now! We can leave before the rest of the house gets up if you hurry."

"Spontaneous, huh?" Buddy yawned.

Caleb bounded out of bed and headed for the shower. "Come on. We can shower together and conserve water."

Buddy threw off the blankets and followed Mr. Conservation into the bathroom.

When they got downstairs, Scout was already padding around the kitchen. He was dressed, with the ubiquitous cup of coffee in his hand.

"What are you two doing up so early? Shit, the birds aren't even awake yet."

Buddy yawned again. "We're going to Tijuana for a few days. What are *you* doing up this early?"

Scout frowned at him. "I've got an appointment."

"At this time of morning? It's not even light out yet."

Caleb hastily poured himself a cup of coffee. "Come on, Bud. Let's go."

Buddy stared at Scout as if he were up to something. "See you in a few days."

"Be careful," Scout called in a loud whisper. "And don't drink the water!"

"What do we do? What do we do?" Buddy was as nervous as a virgin on her wedding night. It was his premiere voyage out of the country, even if it was only across the California-Mexico border.

Caleb laughed. "I've just got to slow down and stop. They're not going to search us for hostages."

The black Bronco eased to a halt. The woman inside the patrol booth waved them through mechanically. Her immediate concern was with one of her press-on nails, which drooped from the end of her most preaxial digit like a tiny pink truce flag, flapping in the wind. The two blond gringos were nothing more to her than a momentary distraction.

Tijuana looked like a war zone; it was an economically depressed area that reeked of poverty. "Is it any wonder they want to come to California?" Caleb said, maneuvering through the streets with easy familiarity.

"Where are we going?" Buddy asked, hanging from the window like a golden retriever, ears to the wind.

"You'll see."

Gravel crunched beneath steel-belted radials as the Bronco skidded down a dirt road, coming to a dust-scattering halt.

Buddy jumped out and stared at the rocky beach and the infinite stretch of the vast Pacific Ocean. He inhaled the fresh salt-air and threw his head back to the bright sun.

"It's not exactly the Tijuana Hilton," Caleb laughed, pulling their gear from the back of the Bronco, "but it's free."

"It's beautiful. And so peaceful." He looked over the campground, which really was nothing more than a dusty parking lot leading down to the beach. Except for a beat up VW van with hippie hieroglyphics painted on the side, they had it all to themselves. "It's great," Buddy exclaimed, "but where do I plug in my hair dryer?"

# 45. Acts of Contrition

Sneaking out of the house before Jesse awoke, Scout inhaled half a dozen cigarettes on route to the AID FOR AIDS PROJECT, which undoubtedly made the Tobacco Lobby light up like nicotine-colored Happy Faces, while simultaneously making the Heart Association clutch their heart-shaped logo. He hadn't been this nervous since he stood at the head of his first English class, facing thirty acne-faced inmates posing as high school students, whose sole intention on being there had less to do with the works of Zora Neale Hurston or Thomas Hardy than with giving him his first nervous breakdown.

Now he was a neophyte of a different color.

Slightly overdressed for his first day at the AIDS Hotline, he nevertheless looked dapper in his Armani trousers and unconstructed Kenzo jacket. He figured if he was going to screw up, he might as well look his best.

There was only one man at the switchboard so early in the morning and he cruised Scout like it was last call at the bar. "The Xerox is in the rear office if you're the repairman," he said in a manly baritone, letting his eyes do the walking.

"I'm not the Xerox repairman."

The man's hands flew swiftly to his denimed hips. His voice rose to its natural tenor. "Well, you're sure as hell not a rapist dressed like *that*, so I suppose any chance of getting ravished is *totally* out of the question!"

Scout was speechless.

"Shit! I'm just *desperate* to get laid, too. I might as well be a nun for all the action I've been getting lately — which is *nil!*"

Silence.

The man folded his arms across his chest, studying Scout. "Listen, honey, I'm not very good at *charades* this time of the morning, so if you're not the repairman, you must be the new recruit." He crossed his legs and pursed his lips. "Well, am I right?"

Scout nodded.

"You got a name, sweetheart?"

Scout swallowed. "Scout."

"*Scout?*" He paused dramatically. "As in *Girl* Scout?"

Scout sensed that this was a complete mistake. "Maybe I'd better come back at another time." Slowly, he began to inch towards the door.

"Relax. I'm not going to steal your cookies!" the man said superciliously.

That seemed debatable.

"I'm Kirk. I'll be training you."

Scout stared at him blankly. Why did his immediate contact with the AIDS Hotline have to be Queen for a Decade? Obviously, karma was at work here.

Kirk patted the chair next to where he was sitting. "How about some OJT? This'll be your command center, so you might as well acquaint yourself with this highly technological equipment." He pointed to the highly technological equipment. "It's called a *telephone* — think you can handle it?"

Scout took a deep breath and sat down.

"These suckers haven't started ringing yet." He sat back and lit a cigarette. "I realize I'm a tad *vivacious*, so try and bear with me. My lover . . . *succumbed* two weeks ago and if I don't keep up this *outrageous* facade, I'll positively *freak!*" He blew a stream of smoke above their heads. "And," he grinned, tapping Scout on the knee, hitching his thumb toward the ceiling, "Scotty absolutely *refuses* to beam me up. And, believe me, with AIDS around, this planet *really* sucks!" he chortled. "Nowadays, I guess it's the only thing that does — if you get my drift? — Talk about Toxic Shock!"

Scout took out a cigarette and relaxed. He even managed a smile.

Kirk reached over and flicked his Bic magnanimously. "*Reality* — ain't it a trip?"

## 46. Horse and Carriage

She looked like a proctologist for Hotpoint: it was a dirty job, but somebody had to do it.

Maizie was on her hands and knees, a red bandanna tied around her hair, an apron over her clothes, rubber Playtex on her hands, with her head stuck inside the oven.

Nash bounded downstairs, gym bag bouncing from his shoulder, and did a comic doubletake. "I felt the same way about Dan Carlton, but believe me — whoever he is, he isn't worth it!"

She withdrew her head from the oven, like a gynecologist from sheeted stirrups. "*What?*"

His eyes widened. "*Aunt Jemima!* — for a second there I thought it was Sylvia Plath."

"Aunt Jemima your *mama!*" she retorted, rinsing a sponge in a pail of water beside her knees. "I hope you realize that this oven hasn't been cleaned since Christ was corporeal. If I hurry, it should be done in time for Thanksgiving!"

Nash shrugged his massive tank-topped shoulders. "I guess it was never one of our highest priorities." He paused, studying Maizie's head. "Say, isn't that my red bandanna?"

"Maybe it is and maybe it isn't. Anyway, I've never seen you actually wear it."

"You don't *wear* it — it's an accessory."

She looked at him like he was crazy. "An *accessory!*"

"Yeah. It's *visual*. You wear it in either back pocket of your jeans, see, depending on ... Well, to distinguish whether you're top or..."

The way she looked at him he might as well have been speaking Swahili.

"See, if you wear it in the left pocket it means..." He chewed his bottom lip. "Forget it, okay? It's dumb anyway. I'm going to the gym."

"I will," she replied, stuffing her head back into the oven.

The veins in Nash's arms and neck stood up like mole tunnels as he s-t-r-a-i-n-e-d to replace the barbell to its original position on the bench press.

Sweat cascaded down the ripples of his sculptured musculature like lilliputian mountain streams. In the distance, two plebes, in color-coordinated gym shorts and tank tops, who had signed away three years of their paychecks in hopes of Herculean physiques, looked on with adulatory amazement.

Noticing them out of the corner of his eye, Nash flexed his drop-dead biceps, then proceeded nonchalantly to the showers.

Inhaling the aromatic essence of male pheromones made the plebes swoon, as did the retreating mountain of male muscles. One of them clutched his chest. "My heart can't take it. I'd give anything to be between the legs of that man."

His companion chuckled. "Poof! You're a jock strap!"

Cars slowed to a crawl on Robertson Boulevard to glimpse the divine specimen of masculinity leaning against the red brick wall of West Hollywood Park.

Waiting for his luncheon date to arrive, Nash was oblivious to the inching m.p.h. parading a few yards before his feet. Instead, his attention was on the latest issue of *Hollywood Tattletales*:

*"Great Ball of Fire: Sparks flew on the set of _____ when its prime time soap queens went for the jugulars. Crew hands had to pry them apart, our 'on-the-set-spy' reports. Obviously, this is one bitch fight we won't see on TV!!!*

*"Hard Times in Locustland dept: What 'Living Legend' was seen*

*hocking her Black Glama Full-Length Mink at a Boys' Town pawn shop???* We won't tell!!!

"*Hold on to your Dodger Caps: It seems our AC/DC anchorman, last seen on the pumped-up bicep of a local gay bartender is now applying for a 'marriage license'? Talk about SWITCH HITTING!! Who does he think he's kidding? Not us!! Don't expect to see Mr. Gay Bartender among the bridesmaids!!*"

As Nash was mulling this tidbit of dirt, a shadow appeared from nowhere.

"What are you reading?"

Nash looked into the handsome face of Dr. Dick Webster. "Trash! Pure trash!"

Dick glanced at the *Hollywood Tattletales* in Nash's hand. "Well, I bet I've got a scoop that's escaped even those muckrakers." His eyebrows shimmied.

He wadded up the scandal sheet and threw it into a park trash receptacle. "What's that?" he smiled.

"Apparently, someone is getting *married*. Guess who was in my office today for a blood test?"

"Barry Manilow?"

Dick laughed. "No."

"Richard Chamberlain?"

"Wrong again. It was that anchorman — Dan Carlton." He shrugged his shoulders. "I thought the news on the grapevine was that he's gay?"

"If he is, it'll be news to his fiancee," Nash grinned, throwing his arm around the doctor's shoulder as they headed up the sidewalk.

# 47. Koyaanisqatsi

Their sleeping bag was soaked, drenched with sweat.

Buddy bolted upright, as if awakening from a nightmare that had him falling off a steep cliff.

Caleb was curled into a tight fetal ball, teeth clattering, shivering with cold sweat.

Buddy wrapped his body around him, holding him tightly. His voice was grave with alarm. "Jesus, you're dripping wet, Caleb. What's wrong?"

Caleb stared at him through blinking eyes. "I'm . . . freezing . . . Bud. I can't . . . stop . . . shaking."

Buddy snatched a beach towel from his knapsack and began rigorously rubbing down his lover's naked, trembling body. Panic surged through him like a broken dam, but he tried desperately to hold back the sweeping terror that consumed his mind. "Is that better, Caleb? Do you feel better now?"

Caleb nodded, shaking like a junkie with the jitters.

Buddy sat him up, wrapping a dry blanket around him while diving for their clothes. "Come on," he said gently, slipping a shirt over Caleb's shoulders, "we're getting out of here!"

After they were both dressed, he loaded the camping gear into the back of the truck and wrapped a blanket around Caleb, placing him in the front seat. Then he jumped into the driver's seat and started the engine. Seconds later, it hit him like a ton of bricks: he didn't know how to drive a stick-shift!

"Jesus, Nash," Scout chided, "put a towel on for christssakes."

Upstairs, Nash passed nonchalantly from the bathroom to his bedroom, with Scout bringing up the rear. "You've seen me naked before. Don't look so shocked. We've all got one."

"Yeah, but they don't all come in the same size. What if Maizie walked up here and saw you like that?"

"She's busy downstairs. Anyway, she's had four husbands. She's not exactly a Pollyanna when it comes to seeing a man naked."

Scout sat down on his bed and thought about it. "I suppose you're right. Anyway, is there anything you need from the market? Toothpaste? Deodorant? K-Y Jelly?"

"Very funny."

"I'm serious. Maizie wants me to pick up some things for Thanksgiving."

Nash thought for a moment. "Get me some toothpaste."

"Okay." Scout got up and started downstairs.

"Hey — and get some K-Y Jelly."

"I knew it," he smirked, calling over his shoulder. "I'll get the giant economy size!"

He had completely forgotten about the grocery strike.

Teamsters were picketing outside the Safeway entrance. The seventeen-day-old strike was getting ugly. One man had been assaulted. Delivery trucks were sabotaged and shot at. Tempers flared and fist fights were rampant, along with name-calling and evil eyes. If looks could kill, shoppers entering the store would have hit the pavement in mass homicide.

Scout looked straight ahead, tunnel-visioning his way past the picketers, some of whom looked like they knew the where-abouts of Jimmy Hoffa.

"*Fruit!*" echoed behind him as he entered, and he had the distinct impression they weren't referring to produce.

Safely inside, he wheeled his cart toward the cookie aisle, nearly mowing down a woman in a nondescript vinyl jacket, jeans, and a post-Eisenhower hairdo that was sprayed stiff and looked like a battling helmet. She fixed him with a furtive stare, then charged down the aisle.

He grabbed a bag of Pepperidge Farm cookies with chocolate mint filling. Obviously, the woman had had the same idea. The bag had already been tampered with, so he finished the job and stuffed a cookie in his mouth, munching from the bag as he wheeled his way to the canned goods.

Maizie had an uneasy feeling in the pit of her stomach. Something was wrong, but she couldn't put her finger on it. The vibes in the air were discordant and portentous. Maybe it was women's intuition, but she had the distinct feeling something was about to hit the fan.

She started to dial Jackson's preschool to see if he was all right when Caleb's Bronco pulled into the driveway like an old steam engine locomotive about to blow, its gears grinding and gnashing like a set of steel dentures, and smoke pouring from the hood like the Second Coming.

"Nash!" she screamed, in a voice that shook the very foundations of the house, then screamed again. *"Nash!!"*

The fierceness of her cry jump-started his adrenaline, causing him to descend the stairs three at a time.

"Something's wrong," she said, and they bolted out the back door with the speed of greased lightning.

Buddy was frantic, shaking like a live wire. His eyes were crazed as he tumbled out of the still-smoldering Bronco.

Maizie steadied him. "Child, what is it? What's wrong?"

"It's Caleb!"

"I'll call the hospital," Nash said, darting back to the house. "What's his doctor's name?"

Shock was setting in. Buddy just stared at him.

"Baby, what's Caleb's doctor's name?" Maizie asked softly. "Can you remember?"

"Dick Webster. Dr. Dick Webster."

After Scout put the grocery bags on the kitchen counter, it took him all of two seconds to surmise that some sort of crisis was at hand. He hadn't seen a look like the one on Jesse's face since he came home from school and his mother told him that his dog Spotty had been splattered. This time, at least, that department was covered — they didn't have a dog.

"What is it?"

"Caleb's in the hospital," Jesse said flatly.

"Jesus! Where's Buddy?"

"Upstairs."

Maizie entered and began fixing a pot of coffee. "Dick Webster just gave him a sedative. He's resting."

A lump caught in Scout's throat. "What happened?"

"Well, as far as we can make out," Jesse replied, "Caleb got sick in Mexico, and Buddy drove them back here. When I got home, they'd already taken Caleb to the hospital in an ambulance."

"Buddy tore up Caleb's Bronco trying to get him here," Maizie added. "Poor thing had never driven a stick-shift before." She shook her head. "I don't know which is worse — the wreck outside or that poor wreck of a boy upstairs."

Buddy felt like the Mafia had fitted him with a pair of cement shoes. His body seemed abnormally heavy, so heavy that the weight descending upon him made it difficult to keep his eyes open.

He wanted to rest — to tune out the world or at least put it on hold for a while until he caught his breath, but even as he began to drift with the velvety tide coursing through his veins, he knew the world did not come equipped with hold buttons or emergency brakes. You took your chances and held on for dear life, even if dear life was sometimes less than cordial and notoriously not so dear, and at times took on the characteristics of a psychotic roller coaster on an expressway to hell. Reality. He had to face reality, even if reality wasn't always "Have a Nice Day!"

Gradually rest came, and Morpheus with it.

In dream, *an elaborate party was in progress at an exotic beach. Guests were dressed in tuxedos and evening gowns, although it was a bright, sunny afternoon. Scout was there, conversing with Truman Capote. Mrs. Cattuzzo, his second grade teacher, applauded as Jerry Falwell balanced precariously above her on a high wire across a secluded lagoon. Maizie was serving bruised fruit from a table of dead sea turtles and caviar as Buddy walked across bright yellow blossoms that lined the beach like a plush carpet. Nobody seemed to notice that he was the only one present without clothes.*

*Presently, the guests gathered at the shoreline. A few feet in front of them was a stake with a long yellow rope connected to it. Everyone was looking out to sea. At the rope's end was a raft, and on the raft was a man, waving frantically to the guests. Everyone waved back, unperturbed that sharks were circling the small craft and that the man on board was in danger.*

*As Buddy started to run into the surf, Nash appeared, pulling up the stake and throwing it out to sea. As the raft drifted further and further out, he realized that the man aboard the raft was Caleb.*

*By this time the guests were laughing, although he fought to make them understand that Caleb's life was in danger. Then Nash pulled him off into the trees to the high grasses. As Caleb disappeared, Nash began licking away his tears, running his hand along the inside of his thighs, caressing his scrotum. He felt ashamed that he responded; that he succumbed; that he hungered for it.*

*When they returned to the crowd, the guests were all gathered at the shore. A school of dolphins had captured their attention as they performed close to the shoreline. Then one of the dolphins jumped into the air, tossing Caleb's heart on to the sandy beach at his feet.*

*When he reached down to pick it up it turned into a beautiful pink conch.*

Maizie eyed Scout suspiciously as he pushed himself away from the table. Nobody had really eaten, they had only picked at their food, but Scout looked especially pallid and uncomfortable.

"What's wrong?" she asked. "Didn't you like it?"

He blinked at her, as if he couldn't focus. "It tasted weird. What kind of chicken was that anyway?"

Nash rolled his eyes. "That kind of chicken was a *fish.*"

"Mine tasted all right," Jesse shrugged.

"So did mine," Dick Webster added.

Scout held his forehead, wobbling slightly as he stood up.

"Are you all right?" Maizie asked. "You look a little funky."

"Child, I *feel* funky." He felt like he was going to vomit.

Jesse looked at him lovingly. "Why don't you take a nap. I think we're all a little tired."

"I think I will. Excuse me."

"There's no *excuse* for you," Nash joked, trying to lighten the mood.

"Fuck you," Scout replied, starting for his bedroom, then somebody turned out the kitchen lights and he collapsed in a heap, like a wino down for the count.

"Jesus, not again!" Nash yelled, jumping to his feet.

Jesse and Dick rushed to his side. "Call an ambulance!" Dick ordered.

Maizie dashed for the telephone, mumbling to herself as she dialed 911: "Damn, it's beginning to look like the last act of *Hamlet* around here!"

## 48. All Through the Night

Roused by the ruckus taking place in the kitchen, Jackson, in Smurfs pajamas, watched in wide-eyed wonder as the paramedics lifted Scout's limp body onto the stretcher.

Jesse felt helpless, watching in silence.

Jackson tugged at his father's trousers. "Is Scout dead, Pop? Did you *kill* him?"

Maizie cupped her hands behind his head and led him back to bed. "Scout's not dead, sugar. He'll be all right, you'll see."

"Come on," Nash said in semi-shock, squeezing Jesse's shoulder, "you can ride with us."

It was early dawn when they returned home.

Maizie, who had fallen asleep on the sofa, woke and put on a pot of coffee, her hair in curlers.

"Is Scout all right?" she asked sotto voce.

"He'll be fine," Dick answered.

Jesse looked tired, but relieved. "Thank God."

"It'll take more than Mercoprop to kill that sucker off," Nash laughed.

"What's that?" Maizie asked.

"Herbicide," Dick said. "The hospital reported several cases of it lately."

Maizie stared at him. "Well, how on earth did he get hold of that?"

"Strikers have been contaminating the supermarkets because the grocery strike is dragging out and people are getting crazy," he said soberly. "We'd better check the rest of the food, Maizie, before anyone in the house eats anything else."

"Well, Christ Almighty!" she snapped, pulling food from the cupboards, "what's wrong with folks nowadays anyway. Poisoning unsuspecting people like that."

Later that afternoon, Scout was discharged.

"How do you feel?" Jesse asked, happy to have his loved one back in one piece.

"Awful!"

"But, Dick said you were better. That you could come home."

Scout pulled down the visor on the passenger's side of the truck, and checked his face in the vanity mirror as Jesse drove them home. "I didn't mean *that*. I feel all right, it's just the indignity of *fainting* in front of everyone. It's so *un*butch!"

"You didn't *faint* — you passed out."

"Well," Scout smiled, looking on the bright side, "at least I had on clean underwear. My mama always warned me about the horrors of skid marks!"

## 49. Scooter

"Come on, Scout. Get up!" Jesse prodded the ball curled up beneath the covers. "Jackson'll be finished with breakfast any minute. Move it!"

Slowly, a wild-child hairdo and sleepy bedroom eyes rose to the occasion. He reached for his glasses and focused on the handsome man at the foot of his bed.

"What time is it?"

"It's time to go, that's what time it is. Let's get it in gear."

He stretched and yawned, then fell backwards against the pillows.

About that time, Maizie popped her head through the bedroom door. "There's a child out here *waiting* to go. Now, if you don't *haul ass*, mister, I'll come in here and do it for you."

He made a face at her. "Shoot, the early bird gets the worm, not the mutt. Besides, I don't feel good."

"Oh, give me a break, Scout. Dick Webster said you were fine and you know it."

"Well, maybe I'm having a relapse!"

"Relapse my ass — now move it or lose it!"

Jesse winked at him. "We'll be outside in the car."

Reluctantly, he got out of bed, calling after his lover. "Jesse, that puppy isn't even going to be awake yet, and you know it!"

Poodles, cute as cotton balls with legs, were pronounced *de trop*. Scout thought they were *too* gay, like mink coats for men, like Emory in *The Boys In The Band*, and high camp. Luckily, Jesse agreed and Jackson passed them by without so much as a wink.

"How about this one?" Jesse said, signaling them over to a pup with a silky sheen of red hair.

Jackson pecked the window. "Yeah, Pop. I like this one."

"Look at this one, Jackson," Scout called. It was a woolly sheepdog pup.

"Yeah, I like this one, Pop!" Jackson exclaimed.

Jesse studied the scampering ball of fur. "It only has *one* eye."

Scout rolled his eyes. "I hope you're joking. That happens to be his *ass!*"

Jesse grinned, pinching Scout's derriere as Jackson ran ahead of them.

The little boy stopped at a cage moments later, and squealed. "That's him, Pop! That's Scooter!"

The puppy barked and licked Jackson's nose through the wire.

"I like this one, Pop!"

The pup knew a sale when he saw one, prancing back and forth inside his cage. The look in his eyes seemed to say: "How much are those people in the window?"

"Ahhh," Scout grinned, "that's the face of Scooter if I ever saw one."

Jesse shook his head. "I don't know. He looks sort of defective to me." He turned toward his son. "Are you absolutely sure? You know you can't change your mind once you get him home."

"Sure I'm sure, Pop. That's Scooter, all right!"


"A *rat!*" Maizie squealed, grabbing for her broom.

"It is not," Jesse laughed. "That's *Scooter!*"

"Is it supposed to look like *that?*"

Scooter followed Jackson around the kitchen and barked; the bark that sounded like a cross between a chipmunk with laryngitis and a baby alligator.

Maizie lowered herself to the floor for a closer look. She shook her head solemnly. "This sucker needs ironing — he's all *wrinkles!*" She poked at him with her finger. "He looks like a little accordion with legs."

"Oh, hush up, girl," Scout chided. "You'll hurt his little feelings."

Scooter barked.

"What'd you do," she sighed, "pick out the ugliest mutt you

could find? He looks like some kind of rodent."

Jesse laughed again, and scratched his chin. "The man at the pet shop said he'd outgrow all those wrinkles."

"Of course he did," Maizie snapped, getting to her feet. "Those fools will tell you anything to make a sale. What's he called, anyway?"

"He's a Shar Pei. He's Chinese."

"Damn," she said, "you couldn't even buy American."

# 50. Hard Times for Lovers

"Holy shit! You scared the bejesus out of me," Scout said, clutching his sweatshirt at the heart.

Buddy looked up and rubbed his eyes. He was at the kitchen table, slumped over a cup of cold coffee.

Scout turned on the overhead light. "Why are you sitting in the dark?" It was still predawn.

"I couldn't sleep."

"Are you all right?" he asked, even though Buddy's face looked like the mask of Tragedy.

Buddy nodded.

"Are you going to see Caleb today?"

He nodded again.

"Well, I'll only be out for a few hours, then I'll stop by the hospital and say hello to Caleb. Maybe we could have lunch together or something."

Buddy's look was noncommital.

"So, I'll see you later." He started out the back door, but turned back. It sounded like Buddy had said something. "What'd you say?"

"Turn out the light, please."

Kirk was on the telephone when Scout, carrying two white styrofoam cups of coffee and a Winchell's Donut box, entered the AID FOR AIDS office.

"No, ma'am," Kirk was saying, "you cannot get AIDS from

drinking out of your hairdresser's Diet Coke can. No ma'am. Nor from hair brushes. No, not from toilet seats, either. That's right. Thanks for calling."

Scout smiled. "Hi. I brought you some breakfast."

Kirk looked inside the donut box. "I sincerely hope you don't think you can buy me off with a couple of chocolate glazes and a cup of coffee."

Scout sat down beside him. "Huh?"

"Don't play possum with me, Girl Scout. You're here less than a week and you're already missing work. Two demerits!!"

"But . . ."

"Actually," Kirk said, arching his eyebrow, "you didn't even bother to *call* — that's another two demerits. Shape up, Girl Scout, or I'll have to take away your Good Citizenship badge. Rip it right off your tits!"

Scout laughed. "Here. I bought you a pack of cigarettes: Macho Marlboro."

"*Sweet Charity!* All is forgiven. You just saved your International Friendship badge." He accepted the cigarettes gracefully. "I really appreciate it. It seems I'm gonna have to start relying on the kindness of semi-strangers."

"What are you *rambling* about?"

"I told myself that if I ever got AIDS, I'd just *diiieee!* Well, it seems that I have — AIDS, I mean."

Scout's face fell. "Don't joke like that."

"Who's joking? I got fired from my full-time job yesterday."

Scout gasped. Jesus, he wasn't joking.

"Honey, they tossed me out like yesterday's news. I'm on the *dole.*"

Scout grabbed his shoulder. "Listen, if there's anything I can do, let me know."

"Oh, it's not so bad. I wanted to lose ten pounds by Christmas, but since I may not be around at Christmas, I'll just eat myself to death." He helped himself to a donut. "Fuck it. At least I won't have to count calories any more."

"Don't," Scout murmured.

"Well, shit, Girl Scout — it's either that or the cigarettes or AIDS. If one of them doesn't kill me, another one will."

Scout drove directly to the hospital after leaving AID FOR AIDS, feeling bewildered and confused by Kirk's revelation. And helpless.

Fear of such impending proportions hadn't invaded the soul of the nation's consciousness since the advent of the A-bomb, which once caused his mama to utter one of her infamous axioms: "Scout, sometimes life is like a shit sandwich, and every day's just another bite!"

It was scary. Now AIDS was vandalizing that consciousness all over again, turning that sandwich into a full-course meal. He wondered, did the banquet ever end?

Scout slammed on the brakes as he passed Tail of the Pup, a fast-food joint shaped like a giant hot dog bun with an equally huge wiener sticking out of each end. Not because he had a sudden craving for junk food, but because Buddy was sitting on the curb crying.

He threw the Volvo into reverse and backed up, then jumped from the car.

"Buddy, what's wrong?"

Buddy, face in hands, didn't answer. He seemed oblivious to everything but his own grief.

Scout sat down beside him, putting his arm around his friend's shoulder. "Bud, what is it?"

"He won't let me see him," he weeped.

"Who won't? Dick Webster?"

He shook his head. "*Caleb!* He told them not to let me in."

"There must be a mistake. Maybe they misunderstood him. Come on. I'll take you back."

"He won't let me in, Scout," he sobbed, handing him a letter from his back pocket.

"What's this?"

"It's from Caleb."

Scout unfolded it, took out the letter and read it:

> Dear Buddy,
> Don't believe everything you hear. I only have the Boys' Town flu — a temperature of 102° and an uncontrollable urge to redecorate! It's that time.
> Love — Caleb

Inside the envelope was a small bundle of crisp bills.

"What's this?" Scout asked.

"He wants me to go away, Scout. To get out of town."

"Why, Bud?"

"Because he wants to *spare* me," he sniffled. "As if I didn't know anything about death. You know I'm not exactly a rookie in *that* department."

Scout gripped the curb as if he'd lost all faith in gravity; as if he no longer trusted the spin of the earth to hold the fabric of life together. Noah, his ex-lover, had taken death on the lam, trying to spare him the pain, too, but from what had Noah actually spared him? He'd still grieved. The pain wasn't lessened. And now Caleb was attempting to do the same thing to Buddy.

"So what are you going to do about it?"

"I don't know. I wish I'd never moved here."

Trusting gravity once again, Scout stood up. "Jesus, you sound like a broken record. Everytime something happens to you, you're ready to pack it in. I've got news for you, kiddo. Life isn't like the movies, with violins filling in space. It's *real*, up close and naked. If you want music, you have to make it yourself."

Buddy stared at him through red-rimmed eyes. "Thanks a lot, Scout. Kick me while I'm down, why don't you."

"Well, shoot, Bud. Life's a long way to run. Sooner or later you're going to have to learn to fight."

"But *how?*"

"Hell, I don't know. You can stop crying for one thing. Didn't you read my article: 'Real Men Don't Cry, They Grow Tumors'? Shoot, pretend you're Tammy Wynette — 'Stand By Your Man.' It worked for her."

A grin was trying to infiltrate Buddy's self-pity.

Scout reached down and pulled him up. "Come on. We'll think of something."

# 51. Meeting of the Minds

It was a *Weight Watchers* nightmare, a glutton's sweet dream.

It was enough to snap the purse strings of the *Frugal Gourmet*,

and reduce Julia Child to spasms of multiple orgasms, while causing Shelley Winters's saliva glands to gush like Niagara Falls.

*Bon appetit* wasn't the half of it. Maizie had Jesse's pickup
truck loaded with every conceivable food substance known to the
free world. She always knocked herself out for Thanksgiving, and
this year, come hell or high water, would be no different. Make
way for *Bon Appetfeast* and a cast of thousands.

Scooter barked as Maizie struggled through the back door carrying two heavy bags of groceries.

"There's a twenty-five-pound turkey out there," she said, "and
I don't think it's going to walk in here by itself."

Scooter scampered around her feet.

"Yeah, I brought you something too, dog, so just cool your
jets." Then, to Nash: "Yo, weight lifter, there's plenty more bags
outside in the truck."

Nash got up from the kitchen table where all the men of the
house were sitting and started toward the back door. Dick Webster started to get up too, but Maizie quickly put him in his place.
"You're still company around here, so park it. *Scout! Jesse! Buddy!*
Do I have to spell it out for you?"

Jesse and Buddy hustled for the door but Scout took his time,
sauntering past her as if his shoes were made of molasses. "I'sa
comin'. I'sa comin'."

Maizie set her bags on the kitchen counter and fixed him
with a haughty glare. "It's not nice to make fun of your *mama* like
that."

Maizie listened intently as the men once more resumed their seats
at the kitchen table.

"I don't know what I can do, Scout," Dick Webster was saying. "But I'll be glad to talk to him."

"Talk to who?" Maizie asked.

"To *whom*," Scout chided. "Talk to *whom?*"

Maizie threatened to lob him with a can of water chestnuts.
"Okay, to *whom*, Mr. Smartass?"

"Caleb," Jesse injected. "Buddy wants to bring him home."

"So, what's wrong with that?" she asked.

"He doesn't want to come," Nash answered.

Maizie's hands shot to her hips. "Well, why on earth not?"

"Because. . ." Buddy started, but Scout cut him off.

"Because he's being *galant*. If you ask me, I think he's seen *Dark Victory* one too many times."

"That's not it, Scout," Buddy protested, "and you know it."

"Then what is it?" Maizie hated being the only one left in the dark (figuratively speaking, of course).

"Well. . ." Scout started, but Maizie abruptly shut him up.

"Child, *please*, let Buddy tell it — Caleb's his friend, not yours!"

Scout crossed his arms across his chest and sank into his chair, causing Jesse to grin to the others. Sometimes his lover acted like a recalcitrant, man-sized version of his son.

So, as the other men listened (Scout with simmering indignation), Buddy told Maizie about Caleb's decision to face his death alone. It wasn't exactly a knee-slapper, but then death rarely was outside of the homicidal antics of Saturday morning cartoon characters that blew up one second and rematerialized in the next frame in a sort of comic-book representation of reincarnation.

"Well," Maizie sighed, "I suppose if that's the way Caleb feels about it, there's not much any of us can do about it."

# 52. Foxy Lady

She had lied through her perfect white teeth.

In fact, she hadn't told a lie of that scale since the wedding night of her first marriage, when her impersonation of a quivering virgin would have sent Meryl Streep back to acting school with her tail tucked between her legs.

"Hey, Sugar," Maizie smiled, flashing every one of her thirty-two teeth. "How are you feeling?"

"Better," Caleb said, returning her smile, albeit not quite matching the vehemence of her pearly whites.

She looked around the hospital room. It seemed to her about as inviting as a back alley on skid row. She removed her hat pin and hat and placed it gently on her lap. "Well now, I suppose you can't wait to get home. You know, I'm fixing a *beautiful* Thanksgiving dinner, with a turkey this big," she bragged, holding her hands up about three feet apart, "with homemade sweet potato pie, pecan pie, pumpkin pie and everything else. And, child, a soul food stuffing that the Indians passed down to my Great Great Grandmother."

Caleb fixed her with a comical smile. "The Indians were into *soul food?*"

"And how," she said breezily. "Shoot, the pilgrims didn't know jack about cookin' until the Indians clued them into herbs and the like. And my Great Great Grandmother was an Indian princess. Child, she passed down secrets Betty Crocker would *kill* for. So, what's say we pack up your stuff and get back to the house. This place is the pits."

Caleb smoothed out his hospital robe. "Oh, it's not so bad."

He might as well have been a pane of glass, and she seemed to be looking right through him. "Caleb, can we cut this Ivy League upper-class heroics routine of yours for just a second and talk turkey?"

"Maizie, I'm a vegetarian," he bluffed.

"You know *exactly* what I mean. Now, you've got a house full of people that love you and you're shacked up here like you don't have a soul in the world that cares a rat's ass about you. I'm going to level with you, Caleb. It just *burns* my ass that you're carrying on this way. It just isn't fair to any of us. And you've got poor Buddy turned every which way but loose. He's just a kid. And, damnit, it's not fair."

"I can't do this to him."

"Then you should have thought about *that* long before you ever got involved with him, Mister. Or with *us!*"

That one stung.

"What do you think we're all here for anyway?" She didn't give him a chance to answer. "I'll *tell* you — We're here to help one another. To give each other hope."

"Hope?"

"That's right. *Hope!* Now, are you going to crawl into some shell like you're a snail or are you going to lean on us a little and live each day that God's given you on this green earth to the fullest?"

"Maybe you haven't noticed, but my days are numbered. And, let me tell you something about hope. I'm dying, Maizie. *Goddamnit, I'm dying!*"

She pulled a hanky from her purse and sat down on the edge of his bed. "I know, darlin'," she murmured, hugging him as if he'd come from her loins. "But you're not dead yet. Not by a long shot. So don't throw away one precious second of what time you do have." Now, she was crying. "Jesus H. Christ, *don't give up!* Hold on to life, honey. Grab it by the short hairs and go down fighting. We'll help you. We'll all help you."

She wiped the tears from his eyes. Then, abruptly, she got up and started rummaging around the room. "Lord, we'll have you out of here in no time."

Caleb sniffled.

Maizie perked right up. "Hallelujah, Lord, it's a brand new day."

# 53. It's a Drag

"I won't do it, Scout. I *won't!*"

"Oh, relax. Jesus, you act like you've never worn a dress in your life."

"I *haven't!*"

Scout was incredulous. "Why not?"

"*Why not?* Because where I come from, men don't wear dresses. What's so peculiar about that?" answered Buddy.

Scout pushed his glasses up his nose. "Come on. *Never?*"

"Never."

"I don't believe it. Every gay person alive has done drag at least *once*. It's a rite of passage."

"Not in Indiana, it's not."

"Well, it's about time you did. Here, put on this wig." He tossed Buddy a scraggly-looking black rat's nest, then continued searching through the box of mismatched garments that a bag lady wouldn't have had the gall to wear. "Here it is," he exclaimed, holding up the cheesy D-cup black lace brassiere. "I wasn't sure if we still had it."

"Are you nuts? I'm not wearing *that!*"

"Why not? Nash wore it once and he's as butch as they come."

"I don't believe you."

"He did! He looked just like Sophia Loren, too."

Buddy found that a bit hard to swallow.

Scout rolled his eyes. "He did! He looked great. Well, not great, but that was only because of his moustache. And then, his cleavage was a little on the hairy side . . . and the tattoo . . . But that was his fault — he should never have gone strapless. Anyway, the *essence* was there."

"I don't care how he looked — I'm not doing it!"

"You want to see Caleb, don't you, and didn't he give specific orders not to admit you?"

"Yeah, but . . ."

"But nothing. Start getting undressed," he ordered, disregarding the feelings of his dragaphobic friend. He reached in the box and pulled out a wrinkled velvet and lamé dress, circa 1950s. The gold lamé was tarnished and the velvet crushed, but Scout was undeterred. "I'll get the iron!"

Buddy looked like a streetwalker from the *Twilight Zone*.

Scout had teased and combed the wig into an outrageous beehive, then topped it with a scarf, tied neatly under Buddy's chin. The dress was a bit on the rumpled side, but Scout convinced his unwilling friend that, "Naturally it's wrinkled. You just flew in from Boston."

"You never should have *ironed* it," Buddy protested, wobbling on masochistic killer heels. "I feel like a fool. And, I look *cheap!*" He did, too — like cheap Christmas trash in November. His make-up looked like it had been applied by Tammy Faye Bakker.

Scout pushed him through the doors of the hospital. "Now, just go up and tell the nurse you're Caleb's sister, and you want to see him."

"Aren't you coming *with* me?"

"Two of us might arouse suspicion."

"I can't, Scout. I just can't."

"Just *do* it!"

"You come with me. I'm not going in there alone."

The nurse at the desk happened to be a male, and he seemed not at all nonplussed by what was confronting him, which appeared to be either an escapee from the psychiatric ward or a bad sex change or a combination of the two.

"May I help you?"

People were beginning to stare, but Scout refused to let it distract him. "We're here to see Caleb Alexander," he said authoritatively. He nodded towards Buddy. "This is his sister. She just flew in from the east coast."

The east coast of *what?* the nurse wondered.

"It's imperative that he ... that *she* sees him."

"Just a moment." After checking the records, the nurse returned to the counter. "I'm sorry, but Mr. Alexander has already checked out."

Scout glanced at Buddy, then back to the nurse. "Are you sure?"

Buddy wanted to die. He could hear people snickering somewhere behind them.

"See," the nurse said, pointing to Caleb's signature.

Scout's eyes rolled heavenward. "Well, that's just great!"

Buddy felt like the prize student in a school for fools.

"Come on." Scout grabbed his hand. "Let's get out of here."

"Have a nice day," the nurse called after them.

"Fuck you!" Scout mumbled beneath his breath.

Buddy jerked his hand away. "Slow down, Scout. I'm going to ... falllll..."

Scout looked back just in time to see Buddy's skirts fly up around his beehived head as he tripped, stumbled, and fell off his high heels. A look of total mortification eclipsed his face.

Buddy was on the floor, like a sniper, shooting beaver to everyone that cared to look. And many did.

His wig askew, pantyhose ripped, pride wounded and ego barely intact, Buddy left the hospital wanting to kill. He wanted to slice Scout's heart out with a double-edged knife. Never in his short life had he ever been so humiliated.

They stalked to the car in abject silence. Then suddenly, from behind, someone called out in their direction.

*"Sisterwoman!"*

Buddy glanced over his shoulder in terror.

"Just ignore him," Scout ordered, looking straight ahead.

Then: "Hey, *Girl Scout!!"*

"Jesus." Buddy was in a frenzy. "He knows you." He panicked. "Give me the *keys!* Give me the *keys!"*

Scout proffered the car keys. Buddy snatched them from his hand and took off in a mad gallop toward the car.

"Hey," Kirk snickered, catching up with Scout, "are the Roller Derby girls in town or is your mama simply on the *shy* side?"

Scout watched as Buddy made his way through the maze of cars. "She'd be better off *on* skates — it takes a certain breed of man to *run* in high heels!"

Buddy was seething when Scout reached the car.

"Why did I ever let you talk me into this? I feel like a complete fool! Everyone was *laughing* at me!"

Scout started the car. "So what? You don't know any of those fools."

"And where's Caleb?" he demanded. *"Where is he?"*

Scout took a deep breath and put the car in drive. Buddy's ranting was getting on his last nerve. "Do I look like Jean Dixon? Chill out! We'll find him."

"How can we *find* him? We don't even know where he is!"

# 54. Mending Fences

Buddy gave new meaning to the words "drag racing."

No sooner had Scout pulled into the driveway (and not soon enough after enduring Buddy's loquacious bitching and moaning all the way home), than Jesse drove in behind him, pulling up behind the Volvo, until their bumpers were practically kissing, guaranteeing no immediate exit for the disheveled passenger caught in woman's clothing.

And, if that wasn't enough to frazzle an already fried demeanor, approaching rapidly on the sidewalk in gym shorts and jogging shoes, all muscle, sweat and hormones, were Nash and Dick Webster.

Buddy freaked. "That's all I need — an *audience!*" He turned to Scout, his eyes all voodoo and revenge. "I'll get you for this one day. I swear it!"

He opened the car door just in time to see Maizie stretching her neck at the kitchen window.

With warp speed, he hitched his dress up around his thighs and streaked to the back door into the kitchen.

Scooter took one look at him, barked threateningly, then hightailed it to the living room where he hid beneath the coffee table.

"What the—" Maizie was all eyes. "Who the hell are *you?*"

Whoever she was didn't answer, but swirled through the kitchen and up the staircase to the safety of higher ground, leaping the stairs three at a time.

Shaking and utterly breathless, Buddy slammed the bedroom door behind him with a resounding bang, then gasped. Resting on the bed was Caleb.

"*Oh, God, no!*" he wailed.

Two startled seconds later, Caleb realized that the woman confronting him was not some cheap B-movie hussy from *Women Behind Bars*, but the young man of his dreams.

Buddy didn't know what to do, so he cried.

Caleb laughed. "Hey, did I miss the party?"

Buddy wouldn't look at him.

"Bud, why are you dressed like that?" he asked, getting up from the bed.

"What are you doing here?" Buddy whimpered. "I thought you were gone."

"Gone? Where?"

"From my life." He tried to pull away, but Caleb held him in a weak hug.

"I'm not running any more. I've been making a real ass of myself lately."

"No you haven't. No you haven't."

"I have, Bud. I was running scared for both of us and I cut

you out of my life. And I'm sorry. But I'm back now, and we're going to make the most of every moment we have together, okay?"

The tears arrived without preamble; impromptu via a wave of emotion. Mascara ran down Buddy's cheeks in black rivulets, like the tears of a tar baby. "Okay?"

"I mean it this time. Are you man enough?"

Buddy hugged him. "I'm man enough."

"Good," Caleb murmured, "then let's get you out of this dress."

It was after one in the morning when Maizie, in robe and slippers, sauntered into the kitchen. "I thought I heard something," she yawned. She slapped the refrigerator with her hand. "For a second there, I thought the turkey was making a run for it."

Scout chuckled. "What are you doing here?"

Her hands shot to her hips. "*Somebody's* got to put the turkey in the oven at five a.m. if Thanksgiving is going to come off on schedule. And I sure as hell don't remember *you* volunteering."

"Well, you're about four hours too early. Want some coffee?"

"No, thank you. I'm going back to bed."

"I'll have some." It was Caleb, bare-chested with pajama bottoms. "I couldn't sleep either."

"I'm glad you're home, Caleb. I'm glad for Buddy and I'm glad for you. He's crazy about you."

Maizie lingered a moment, listening and watching.

"I know he is. And I know everyone in this house cares about me, too."

"You got that right," Maizie smiled, then made her exit as Scooter waddled in, stretched and yawned, then stared at them as if they were fools for being up so early.

Scout reached down and scooped him up, snuggling the pup against his chest. "You know, I've always wanted a family, and now I feel like I have one. And, all under one roof."

# 55. Thanksgiving

Homemade pies cooled on a wire rack.

Maizie buzzed around the kitchen like a frenzied finalist in the Betty Crocker Bake-Off. It was eighty degrees outside. Inside, the kitchen felt like an aromatic sauna. The turkey had an early bird call of five a.m. and had been in the oven awaiting its place of honor on the table.

Maizie was cooking on four burners, assiduously stirring and tasting from four different pots. The kitchen smelled like a mouth-watering gourmet dream. All that was missing was the pilgrims and Indians.

Scout was on the kitchen extension. "Just get your skinny white . . . *what?* Will you give me a break? Put that tired-ass turkey dinner back in the freezer and get over here. You're *having* Thanksgiving dinner with us, and I will not take no for an answer."

"Who's that?" Maizie asked.

"It's a friend of mine," Scout answered, "and," he continued into the telephone, "he's having dinner with us! *Good-bye!* I'll see you in a few minutes."

As Scout hung up, Nash appeared from upstairs.

"Well, well," Scout sneered, "if it isn't Mr. Takes a Lickin' and Keeps On Tickin' himself. Jesus, don't you two ever come up for air? You've surely reached sexual *satori* by now.

Maizie glanced over her shoulder. "You jealous or just complaining?" she teased good-naturedly.

"Neither," he countered. "Just stating facts." Then to Nash, "I assume Dick will be coming down shortly?"

"He's in the shower."

"Good," he smiled, grabbing an extra plate from the cupboards and heading outside.

Nash helped himself to a cup of coffee, groggily scratching his chest. "You been up long?" he asked.

Maizie licked a wooden spoon. "Honey, we've been up for hours. Scout's been decorating the patio all morning. Buddy and Caleb's been setting the table, and Jesse's been keeping Jackson out of my hair. You're the only one that's not lifting a finger for this shindig."

Nash threw his hands up in the air. "*Ex-cuuusssseee* me!"

"Shoot, it's the truth," she teased. "You'd better get the spirit and pitch in, too, fool. And that goes for your doctor friend, too! This dinner ain't waitin' for nobody."

"That's subtle, Maizie. Really subtle." He started toward the stairs, a cup of coffee in each hand. "We'll be down in a few minutes."

Scout, in a flaming fuchsia Moss Brown Hawaiian-print shirt of vertically climbing orchids, Caribbean blue shorts, and striped espadrilles, was living proof that all gays are born with an innate sense of decor and design. His knowledge of the basic fundamental concepts of line and space and the effects thereof, were nil.

The patio had been transformed into a schizophrenic pastiche of high tech, Sears Roebuck, bamboo, twinkling Christmas tree lights, vivaciously strung Chinese paper lanterns, and — courtesy of Jackson — one hanging coconut head. He had single-handedly transformed the patio into a cheesy optical illusion of which only the blind were spared.

"Have a beer," Nash whispered to Dick. "Maybe it'll help."

"It'll look better once the sun goes down and the Christmas tree lights are turned on," Buddy shrugged. "I think."

Nash shook his head. "This settles it."

"Settles what?" Dick asked.

"That all of Scout's taste is in his mouth."

Jesse sneaked up behind him. "Hey, I heard that."

Nash glanced over his shoulder. "Did he do all of this blindfolded? It's a nightmare!"

"Well," Caleb injected, "if it's any consolation, I saw Jackson helping him."

Nash shook his head. "That explains one thing. Jackson must be heterosexual — *they* can't decorate either!"

Presently, Kirk arrived. Scout made the introductions, saw to it that he had a cocktail, and ushered him out the back door to the patio where a picnic table was set like a banquet table.

Kirk surveyed the area with great care, taking every nuance

in with appraising eyes, then turned to Scout, full face. "Who was your decorator — *Ronald McDonald?*"

Maizie had outdone herself.

"Hmmm, looks great." Scout rubbed his hands together as Nash lifted the turkey on to the elegantly sheathed table.

"Now," Maizie said, the matriarch of a full table of men, "who's going to say grace?"

Everyone quickly exchanged glances. They *never* said grace.

"I will," Scout volunteered.

Maizie started to bow her head, but Scout wasn't quite finished.

"Actually, it's more of a toast." He squeezed Jesse's thigh beneath the table while holding up his glass with his free hand.

Glasses shot into the air.

"First of all," Scout smiled, "here's to good friends!"

Kirk rolled his eyes. "Oh, God. He's going to sing the Michelob theme song!"

Maizie cackled. She reached over and patted Kirk on the thigh. "I like you, honey. You're welcome here any time."

"Sing it, Scout!" Nash laughed.

He fixed Kirk with a threatening stare that carried no threat at all. "I'm *not* going to sing!" He cleared his throat. "As I was saying, here's to good friends, to this Thanksgiving occasion that enables us to celebrate that friendship, and to this beautiful feast Maizie has prepared for us. . ."

"Here, here!!" echoed around the picnic table.

"*And,*" Scout continued, "to life, love and happiness!"

"Right on!" Maizie exclaimed, "and *Amen!* Happiness is at this address!"

"Amen," Nash and Dick echoed.

"Amen!" Kirk exclaimed.

"Amen," Jackson giggled.

Scooter, salivating for some turkey, barked.

Caleb squeezed Buddy's knee furtively beneath the tablecloth, their eyes reflecting each other's images. "Amen!"

Jesse hugged Scout's shoulder. "Well done."

Surprisingly enough, as dusk fell the Christmas tree lights *did* subdue the garishness of the patio. So did the champagne, which flowed like an eternal spring at a bacchanalian orgy.

"Here," Maizie said, shoving another piece of sweet potato pie in front of Scout.

"No way." He patted his belly. "I feel like a float in Macy's Thanksgiving Parade."

"Shoot!" Maizie snorted. "I'll eat it myself."

Kirk and Jesse began clearing the table, with Scout soon joining in.

Caleb and Buddy pecked Maizie on the cheek, then headed inside to rest. "Great dinner, Maizie."

She beamed for a second, then called to Scout. "And, put *Aretha* on the stereo. This mood music is driving me to distraction."

"Yes, ma'am," he called over his shoulder.

"I'll do it," Nash injected.

Maizie eyed him with the disbelieving stare of an IRS auditor. "It's about time you did something," she mumbled, winking at Dick Webster.

Nash matched her stare. "And stop making eyes at my man!"

"It don't hurt to look," she shot back. "And bring out the coffee when you return."

Jesse played Old Maid with Jackson on the patio as Scout and Kirk started on the dishes.

"Is Caleb the one you told me about?" Kirk asked.

Scout nodded, handing him a plate to dry. "It's sad, huh?"

"This whole thing is sad. Sad and scary. AIDS has suddenly reinvented sin."

Scout didn't understand. "Why do you say that?"

"Because this disease is going to bring down the clamorous wrath of the Jerry Falwells and Pat Robertsons and God knows who else. Love is suddenly fatal, and you *know* this is just what the fanatics have been waiting for."

"Oh, God, I hope you're wrong."

"So do I."

Caleb and Buddy were upstairs napping.

Jackson had fallen asleep on his father's knee.

The rest of the house gathered in the living room.

"It'll be time to get out the Christmas decorations pretty soon," Scout said to no one in particular.

"Get them out?" Nash grinned. "You've already gotten them out. All you have to do is move them *inside!*"

Scout stared at him. "Read my lips!"

"My parents called already and asked what I wanted for Christmas," Kirk smiled. "I told them a new immune system — they thought it was something for my *car!*"

Maizie smiled solemnly. "You're welcome to spend Christmas with us, Kirk."

"Yeah," Scout added. "You're practically one of the family now."

"Yeah," Jesse grinned, "you'd better believe him, too. If it's up to Scout, he'll add another wing to the house so you can move in with us."

Dick Webster patted Scooter's bulbous belly. "I think I'll sell my place and move in, too. You guys have a great family here."

Nash's expression at this revelation contained a hint of benediction. "Do you really mean it? I mean, you would do that for me?"

"Well, I haven't exactly been asked."

Maizie rolled her eyes. "You mean to tell me you haven't asked him, *yet?*" She winked at the handsome doctor, then turned her gaze back to Nash. "Honey, you'd better grab him before *I* ask him to move into *my* place."

Everyone laughed. But to Scout, it seemed like a puzzle and all the pieces were finally coming together to complete a picture. His heart seemed to glow inside him like E.T.'s. He wished it could always be like this. One big happy family.

# 56. Love Talks

Never mind how Love begins, where it comes from, how it got here, or how long it intends to stay.

Nothing applies.

Such questions are irrelevant and tend only to complicate the Due Process of Love.

Again, nothing applies.

Like a vagabond, Love travels unencumbered, without baggage or major credit cards.

Like a politician, Love sometimes promises more than it delivers.

Like a bandit, Love has its own ways and means.

Like a hobo, Love gets here when it arrives.

Nothing applies.

Searching for answers is futile. You can issue a subpoena, drag Love to court, but you can't make it talk. Love pleads the Fifth Amendment.

Skilled as a magician's hand is, Love is still quicker than the eye. Now you see it; now you don't. Love is a prestidigitator extraordinaire. A terrorist of the heart. A hijacker. A hit-and-run driver. A master of disguises. And you don't need a passport to be taken prisoner or to be held captive. Love knows no rules.

But the real question on everyone's lips is: Where does Love go when it leaves (the Heartbreak Hotel)?

How does it get there (here) without directions or a Rand McNally?

Does Love have a forwarding address?

And, more importantly, will Love pass this way again?

Wolves and Canadian geese mate for life. So do hawks. Sometimes, though it seems more and more infrequently, homo sapiens do too.

Scout deYoung wanted to *Love* for life, but in the gay community, as well as the heterosexual community, and quite possibly all communities within the gravatational pull of the global village, that seemed impossible to pull off. Maybe Houdini could, but he was nowhere to be found.

There had to be calm after emotionally stormy seas when lovers bailed out or jumped ship completely.

There had to be dry land after the turbulence of sad-eyed Romeos too afraid to plunge into a brimming sea of commitment.

Scout deYoung had learned to roll with the punches. Love was finally paying sweet dividends.

"I never wanted much," he'd sighed, "but I've always needed an awful lot."

"A lot," Love replied, "is exactly what I have to give."

Scout adjusted his glasses. "Can I get *that* in writing?"

Love mused profusely. "I don't come with any written guarantees or five-year warranties or whichever comes first! You throw the dice and take your chances like everyone else."

"Are you telling me Love is a *crap* shoot?"

"Hey," Love cautioned, "you take the bitter with the sweet. I never promised you a rose garden."

"If it was a rose garden I was after, I would have become First Lady!" Scout countered.

Love appreciated a sense of humor. "Then, what are you bitchin' about? It's better to have lost in Love than to never have Loved at all. Loosen up, chump."

"*What?*" The vote was in. Love was not above cheap sentiment.

"Wake up and smell the cappuccino, buster!" Love smiled wryly, imitating a Caravaggio Cupid. "'Love is like an onion: you peel it off one layer at a time, and sometimes you weep.'"

"You're not only trite, but a plagiarist as well. You nicked that from Carl Sandburg."

Love, pretty in pink, blushed three different shades.

"*And*, Sandburg was talking about *life*, not Love!"

"Semantics! Semantics! Why split hairs — it's all the same thing, isn't it? Love is synonymous with *life* and versa vice," Love chuckled. "As if *you* didn't already know that. Besides, you have to kiss a few toads before you find a prince. The debris comes with the territory."

Scout slapped his forehead. "But when does it all end?"

"There is no end until it ends, that's when."

"Are you for real?"

"Does time stand still?" Love's mouth was full from munching on an afternoon valentine. "Well..."

"No, but..."

"Listen, kiddo, this carpenter is the real thing this time — the last exit on the Freeway of Love. Don't fuck it up!"

"How eloquent."

Love licked it's rosy fingertips; picked its teeth with Cupid's arrow. "This is from the *gut*," Love enunciated. "I leave the fandango and dappled dreams to you writers, so when you get around to writing that book of yours, mention my name. I need all the publicity I can get!"

Scout chuckled. "I will. I promise."

"Preferably *above* the title, if you don't mind."

Love went unheard. Scout was thinking about something else. "What about Nash? And Buddy?"

Love peered over the rims of its Lolita-shaped, rose-colored glasses. "I'm not a bleeding fortune teller, but the Queen of Soul once said: 'Keep on lookin' and just keep on cookin'.' Tell Nash it's time to take the pot off the stove and keep his best recipe in his jeans for a while. This doctor fellow just might be the cure he's been looking for without even realizing he's been looking. These are definitely hard times for lovers."

"And, Buddy?"

Love removed the rose from its teeth. "That's a tough one, all right. Let me see..."

Scout waited as Love pondered.

"Well, I wish I could quote Fitzgerald since Hemingway is a little too butch even for my tastes, but old Ernest pretty much hit the nail on the head when he said, 'All stories end in death, and he is no true-story teller who would keep that from you.' Get my drift?"

Unfortunately, Scout did.

"The passion play may end, but Love lives on. He'll Love again, in time, if he doesn't let this one blind him to my glory. I am," Love boasted, "*eternal!*"

Scout still looked saddened.

"Just remember," Love smiled, "*J'aime et j'espere* — I Love and I hope. Pass it on."

# 57. Tempus Fugit

Having a "White Christmas" was about as likely as a three-legged horse winning the Triple Crown, but that minor detail didn't deter the forever young heart of Scout deYoung, who as a child in

Rhode Island had experienced enough "White Christmases" to last his sinuses a lifetime, thank you.

So what if the snow-encased picture window had been artificially produced with a can of fake snow? So what if Jack Frost couldn't get a visa beyond the Mason-Dixon line? So what if Frosty the Snowman, posturing incongruously on the front lawn, was made of durable plastic and not the real McCoy? So what if his rosy-colored cheeks got their glow from a 75-watt bulb? Big deal. A mere geographical technicality. Christmas without the meteorological phenomena of various crystalized tabular and columnar precipitation was still Christmas. So much so, that Scout had badgered his lover into driving him and Jackson and Scooter in the pickup to the train yards in downtown Los Angeles, to purchase one of the very first Christmas trees to be unloaded in December.

By nightfall of the same day the tree was strung with decorations, lighted and twinkling, heralding the rapid approach of St. Nick, his reindeer and any other fortuitous event that might want to crash land into the tableau of holiday festivities.

Gertrude Stein knew whereof she spoke when she uttered: "Buying is more American than thinking."

In a consumer society which thrives on spending beyond its means, perhaps only a Pythagoras or an Einstein could decipher the square root of Scarlett O'Hara Economics (I'll think about the national deficit tomorrow) that keeps this great country afloat.

Then again, perhaps not. Ms. Stein seemed to have an uncanny grasp of the old voodoo economics thesis, and although she'd been called many names in her life, mathematician was not among them.

Whatever she may have been called, Scout embraced her philosophy in more ways than one, but most assuredly with an open wallet, as if he alone, singlehandedly, like Atlas, could keep the frazzled head of commerce above water. Department stores nuzzled him to their collective bosoms.

But there was also a method to his spending madness that lasted through Christmas, into post-Christmas sales and on into the New Year, which perhaps only those closest to him could comprehend. Spending was one way to help him forget the Thanksgiving picture etched in his mind's eye: a table of men who had eclipsed friendship and become his family. A picture frozen in time and space. A perfect memory of happiness in an imperfect world. A brief moment before Life pitched one of its famous knuckleballs that zoomed over the horizon like a funked-out kamikaze pilot from hell, looking for a direct hit, proving once again that Mama, in her inimitable way, was right:

"Son, sometimes Life is like putting lipstick on a pig — it still doesn't hide the ugliness underneath!"

Or as Scout remarked after Caleb's death: "Life's fairy tales can have happy endings, but sometimes even fairy tales are Grimm."

# 58. Postscript

Dick and Nash held their noses as they came downstairs.

Kirk and Jesse were at the kitchen table trying to enjoy a morning cup of coffee.

"Jesus, what's that *smell?*" Nash exclaimed.

Maizie eyed him suspiciously. "It's the same thing you smelled yesterday and the day before. *Cabbage!*"

"Not *again!* Damn, how long does this rite continue? You've even got me dreaming about those stupid vegetables!"

Maizie stirred the pot with a huge wooden spoon. "Two more days by my calculations, then this house is blessed with prosperity for a new year."

Kirk wrinkled his nose. "It smells like a field of cabbages got together and farted!"

"You hush up," Maizie warned. "Who knows — maybe Scout will win another sweepstakes and buy me a Mercedes."

"Where is he anyway?" Nash asked, trying not to gag.

"He's in the study," Jesse smiled, containing an uncontrollable urge to laugh. "Probably burning incense."

"Oh, he is not," Maizie remarked, ignoring their comments. "He's writing to Buddy."

"Well, I'm going somewhere it doesn't stink of cabbages." He grabbed his companion's arm. "Come on, Dick — Let's go outside and breathe the smog!"

Maizie wagged her spoon at him, one hand on her hip. "Make fun of me, but this is the smell of *prosperity!* My mother swore by this method, and she was *solvent!!*"

Kirk rolled his eyes. "Wait for me!"

"And where do you think you're going?" she asked.

Mimicking her, his hands shot to his nonexsistent hips. "To prepare for my interview with *God* — all right?"

Maizie grinned. "Child, you should quit — you're too bad!"

Nash and Dick threw their arms around him. "Come on, Champ. You can walk with us."

Jesse padded into the study with a fresh cup of coffee for his lover. "Hey, handsome, what are you doing?"

Scout looked up from his typewriter. "I'm going to start on my book this morning after I finish this letter to Buddy."

Jesse settled in the old beat-up chair, patting his thighs. Scout willingly accepted the invitation, a sucker for any hues of romance, bringing the letter with him.

"Can I read it?"

"Sure." Scout handed it to him, watching Jesse's face as he read:

Dear Bud,

Have your balls turned *blue*, yet?? Jesus, *21* below zero! — give me break!

We were all happy to hear that you finally met someone, even if, as you say, it's "nothing serious." Sometimes company is the best remedy. I do have one question though: Where on earth did you meet a gay-activist-priest in Indiana? But more importantly — does the Pope know?

While we're on the subject of couplings, listen to this. Guess who's getting married? Give up? Gutter Girl aka Nash and Dick Webster!! We're going to have a doctor in the family. I still find it hard to believe that the tramp has settled down. We're planning a June wedding at the house *only*, Nash insists, if I promise *not* to decorate. Is the Bitch ungrateful or what? And this from a man who thinks his trousseau should contain at least one *leather* ensemble.

Holy Shit!! A terrific idea just flashed into my mind. Since you already mentioned that you and the renegade priest are planning a visit in the summer, *he* can officiate! Isn't that a great idea? I can't wait to tell Nash and Dick — and the *Pope* — he'll shit!! I'm sure it'll be a first for the Catholic church.

Now, for the DIRT! Or as Maizie says: "Put on your aprons — mud will be slung tonight!" Enclosed is a clipping from the *L.A. Times*. Recognize that face? Well, you should. He didn't make the front page, but I guess it's official — Dan Carlton tied the knot — to a *real* woman. The gossip in Boys' Town is buzzing over this one. Seems he's already been spotted with another man. Obviously, he's not taking his vows seriously. I'll tell you this, he's not fooling anyone, probably not even the bride. Like I always said: Once a closet queen — always a closet queen!!

Now, the good news. Kirk has reconciled with his family. They're taking him in, so he'll be moving back to Texas soon. I know he's in your prayers, too.

Thank God for the New Year. It feels like a shiny light is finally breaking through the storm to new beginnings. We're all looking forward to your return. Your old room is always ready.

Take care. I know in my heart, you're going to be all right. These things take time.

Love & Kisses—

Scout

Jesse gave his main man a solid squeeze. "What about the book?"

"Jesus, give me a break — I only have two hands."

"Well, have you written anything, yet? Does it have a title?" He hedged. "Am *I* in it?"

Scout grinned. "We're all in it. Naturally, I'll have to whitewash the characters to protect the guilty."

Jesse goosed him.

Scout jumped up squealing. "Do that again and I'll dedicate the book to you."

Jesse was about to grab him when Maizie's head popped through the study door. She shook her head. "Are you two at it *again?*"

They grinned guiltily.

"Well, put it on hold. Scout, your mama's on the phone."

He ran for the kitchen extension.

Maizie and Jesse hurried to the desk. "Hurry," she coaxed. "We don't have much time."

Jesse was already going through the papers scattered about the desk. "Relax. They always talk for days."

Maizie picked through the papers. "He'll kill us if he catches us."

"Hey," Jesse whispered, nudging her. "I think this is it." He pulled a pad of yellow foolscap from the desk drawer. "He always writes on this first."

Maizie lurched for it. "Is there anything about *me?*"

"Hey, I sleep with him," Jesse laughed, snatching it back. "I want to see what he writes about *me!*"

They hovered over the desk like Soviet spys, searching for clues.

Maizie looked disappointed. "Shoot, these are just notes."

"Wait a second." Jesse scanned the longhand. "This must be the title."

"Read it," Maizie threatened. "Read it!"

Jesse cleared his throat. "*Boys' Town. . .*"

Maizie rolled her eyes. "Well, that's *original!*"

He elbowed her, then started again: "Fairy tales *can* have happy endings, but sometimes even fairy tales are Grimm."

"I get it," Maizie snickered. "It's a play on words."

Jesse continued: "Once upon a time there was an enchanted grotto in a small section of West Hollywood, known as Boys' Town. . ."

Ten percent of the author's royalties for this work
are being donated to the American Foundation for AIDS
Research in Los Angeles, California.

# Other books of interest from
# ALYSON PUBLICATIONS

*Don't miss our FREE BOOK offer at the end of this section.*

☐ **THE TWO OF US,** by Larry Uhrig, $7.00. The author draws on his years of counseling with gay people to give some down-to-earth advice about what makes a relationship work. He gives special emphasis to the religious aspects of gay unions.

☐ **SEX POSITIVE,** by Larry Uhrig, $7.00. Many of today's religious leaders condemn homosexuality, distorting Biblical passages to support their claims. But spirituality and sexuality are closely linked, writes Uhrig, and he explores the positive Biblical foundations for gay relationships.

☐ **HOT LIVING: Erotic stories about safer sex,** edited by John Preston, $8.00. The AIDS crisis has encouraged gay men to look for new and safer forms of sexual activity; here, over a dozen of today's most popular gay writers erotically portray those new possibilities.

☐ **TO ALL THE GIRLS I'VE LOVED BEFORE, An AIDS Diary,** by J.W. Money, $7.00. What thoughts run through a person's mind when he is brought face to face with his own mortality? J.W. Money, a person with AIDS, gives us that view of living with this warm, often humorous, collection of essays.

☐ **DANCER DAWKINS AND THE CALIFORNIA KID,** by Willyce Kim, $6.00. Dancer Dawkins would like to just sit back and view life from behind a pile of hotcakes. But her lover, Jessica Riggins, has fallen into the clutches of Fatin Satin Aspen, and something must be done. Meanwhile, Little Willie Gutherie of Bangor, Maine, renames herself The California Kid, stocks up on Rubbles Dubble bubble gum, and heads west. When this crew collides in San Francisco, what can be expected? Just about anything. . . .

☐ **DEAR SAMMY: Letters from Gertrude Stein and Alice B. Toklas,** by Samuel M. Steward, $8.00. As a young man, Samuel M. Steward journeyed to France to meet the two women he so admired. It was the beginning of a long friendship. Here he combines his fascinating memoirs of Toklas and Stein with photos and more than a hundred of their letters.

☐ **SAFESTUD: The safesex chronicles of Max Exander,** by Max Exander, $7.00. "Does this mean I'm not going to have fun anymore?" is Max Exander's first reaction to the AIDS epidemic. But then he discovers that safesex is really just a license for new kinds of creativity. Soon he finds himself wondering things like, "What kind of homework gets assigned at a SafeSex SlaveSchool?"

☐ **COMING OUT RIGHT, A handbook for the gay male,** by Wes Muchmore and William Hanson, $6.00. The first steps into the gay world — whether it's a first relationship, a first trip to a gay bar, or coming out at work — can be full of unknowns. This book will make it easier. Here is advice on all aspects of gay life for both the inexperienced and the experienced.

☐ **ONE TEENAGER IN TEN: Writings by gay and lesbian youth,** edited by Ann Heron, $4.00. One teenager in ten is gay; here, twenty-six young people tell their stories: of coming to terms with being different, of the decision how — and whether — to tell friends and parents, and what the consequences were.

☐ **SOCRATES, PLATO AND GUYS LIKE ME: Confessions of a gay schoolteacher,** by Eric Rofes, $7.00. When Eric Rofes began teaching sixth grade at a conservative private school, he soon felt the strain of a split identity. Here he describes his two years of teaching from within the closet, and his difficult decision to finally come out.

☐ **KAIROS: Confessions of a Gay Priest,** by Zalmon O. Sherwood, $7.00. "Gay" and "priest" are words which seldom appear together in public, but are often whispered in the same breath. In *Kairos* Zal Sherwood shares the ordeal he faced as a gay man who refused to hide behind his clerical collar.

**EIGHT DAYS A WEEK**

a novel by
**Larry Duplechan**

## Get this book free!

Can Johnnie Ray Rousseau, a
22-year-old black singer, find
happiness with Keith Keller, a
six-foot-two blond bisexual jock
who works in a bank? Will Johnnie Ray's manager ever get him
on the Merv Griffin show? Who
was the lead singer of the
Shangri-las? *Eight Days a Week*,
by Larry Duplechan, answers
these and other silly questions,
while telling a love story as
funny, and sexy, and mem-
orable, as any you'll ever read.

If you order at least three other books from us, you may request a FREE
copy of this entertaining book. (See order form on next page.)

---

☐ **THE LAVENDER COUCH,** by Marny Hall, $8.00. Here is a
guide to the questions that should be considered by lesbians or gay men
considering therapy or already in it: How do you choose a good ther-
apist? What kind of therapy is right for you? When is it time to leave
therapy?

☐ **REFLECTIONS OF A ROCK LOBSTER: A story about growing
up gay,** by Aaron Fricke, $6.00. When Aaron Fricke took a male date to
the senior prom, no one was surprised: he'd gone to court to be able to
do so, and the case had made national news. Here Aaron tells his story,
and shows what gay pride can mean in a small New England town.

☐ **GAY AND GRAY,** by Raymond M. Berger, $8.00. Working from
questionnaires and case histories, Berger has provided the closest look
ever at what it is like to be an older gay man. For some, he finds, age has
brought burdens; for others, it has brought increased freedom and
happiness.

☐ **TALK BACK! A gay person's guide to media action,** $4.00. When were you last outraged by prejudiced media coverage of gay people? Chances are it hasn't been long. This short, highly readable book tells how you, in surprisingly little time, can do something about it.

## To get these books:

Ask at your favorite bookstore for the books listed here. You may also order by mail. Just fill out the coupon below, or use your own paper if you prefer not to cut up this book.

**GET A FREE BOOK!** When you order any three books listed here at the regular price, you may request a *free* copy of *Eight Days a Week*

— — — — — — — — — — — — — — — —

Enclosed is $_____ for the following books. (Add $1.00 postage when ordering just one book; if you order two or more, we'll pay the postage.)

1. _____

2. _____

3. _____

4. _____

5. _____

☐ Send a free copy of *Eight Days a Week* as offered above. I have ordered at least three other books.

name: _____

address: _____

city: _____ state: _____ zip: _____

### ALYSON PUBLICATIONS
Dept. H-26, 40 Plympton St., Boston, Mass. 02118

**This offer expires Dec. 31, 1990.** After that date, please write for current catalog.